COWBOYS
Gay Erotic Tales

COWBOYS
Gay Erotic Tales

EDITED BY TOM GRAHAM

CLEIS
PRESS

Published in the United States by Cleis Press Inc., P.O. Box 14697, San Francisco, California 94114.

Printed in the United States.
Cover design: Scott Idleman
Cover photograph: Thomas Watkin
Text design: Frank Wiedemann
Cleis logo art: Juana Alicia
First Edition.
10 9 8 7 6 5 4 3 2

Hank Edwards' "Gold Rush" originally appeared in a slightly different form under the title "Miner Sixty-Niner" in *Bear* magazine (November 2000). Dominic Santi's "Urban Cowboys" originally appeared in a slightly different form in *Honcho* magazine (May 2001).

Contents

INTRODUCTION

I grew up on a ranch in Wyoming, where I learned how to herd cattle as well as ride and rope like nobody's business. My youthful years taught me to be fiercely independent and to only ask for help when necessary, but also to take risks whenever the opportunity presents itself. As I grew into a wild teenager, the excitement of ranch life shifted in a new direction for me. Suddenly I was less interested in ridin' horses and ropin' cattle than I was in ridin' and ropin' the masculine, sweaty, muscular ranch hands my parents employed. Guys with names like Ry and Troy and Jackson. Guys with tight bodies wrapped in flannel and worn Wranglers.

Though once or twice my ranch-hand fantasies turned to reality (thank you, Cooper), rural Wyoming offered little promise of my experiencing a full, fun sex life. So off to Chicago I went, to earn a college degree and troll the bars of Boys Town. There I grew into a man—in more ways than one. I stayed in the Windy City for years, where I met my partner Evan, but something was lacking. I missed the wide-open land, the smell of middle-of-nowhere air, the friendly way men tipped their hats to me and said, "Howdy, boy."

It took a lot of convincing to get an Ivy Leaguer like Evan to up and move with me back to Wyoming, but over time he got used to the idea. We've been here nearly five years, and we've both forgotten all about city life. In fact, we love to dress up and play cowboy with each other. Sometimes I'll be the wanted man and Evan the small-town sheriff. Or he'll play the naïve ranch hand while I'm the tough-as-nails property boss, making sure he follows my instructions to the *T*. My favorite "event," though, is rodeo night, and I must say, Evan has sure learned some high-falutin' ropin' tricks over the past five years.

What is it about cowboys that turns gay men into lusty pigs? Is it their bristly jaws? Well-honed bodies? Seductive swagger? Their wild abandon? All of the above and more. And let me tell you, there's nothing in the world like a sexy cowboy mounting another cowboy. In this fiery collection, you find all this and more. Hot, well-crafted stories of rollicking bunkhouse orgies, dirty backroom hookups in country-western bars, and young, hung buckaroos wrangling each other. In these pages, duels occur not on the streets but between the sheets, and the maverick writers in this book take you on a hot and heavy, no-holds-barred trip through the Old West to the New West, where *ramrod, six-shooter,* and *hog-tied* take on entirely new meanings.

So take off your chaps, cowboys, and hang up your spurs. We're going for one helluva long, hot, dirty ride.

Tom Graham

A HEART FULL OF SCARS

Hank Edwards

The wind is relentless, sweeping up snow and bits of dirt as it screams through town. Martin's house, on the rise at the end of the settlement, receives the full brunt of it. The windows rattle in their panes, and he hears the clatter of the gate out front.

Biscuit raises his head and whines quietly.

"It's all right, boy," Martin assures him. "Just the wind."

The dog thumps his tail twice then lowers his shaggy yellow head. Martin turns from the novel he's attempting to read and looks out the window at the snow. It's starting to fall faster. From his chair he sees the sheriff's station and the flickering glow of Dalton's oil lamp through the window. He wonders whether Dalton is looking up the hill at the same moment, thinking of him.

He tries to return his attention to what he's reading, but he's lost track of the story and all the characters remind him of Dalton. Abandoning the book, he stares into the fire and lets his mind go where it wants.

They had met several months ago, Dalton a small-town sheriff and Martin a young doctor fresh out of school and looking to put down roots. Dalton had been the first to welcome him to town, and as fate would have it he turned out to be his first patient.

It was late spring, 1903, and the sky arched blue and serene overhead, stretching far and wide across the flat prairie land. Martin had just taken the last box of his belongings off the wagon when he heard a horse approaching. Turning, he squinted against the late-afternoon sun at the rider coming up the low rising hill to the fence that marked Martin's yard. The man sat straight and tall in his saddle, his long legs clutching the sides of his horse with ease.

"Afternoon," Martin called. "Help you?"

The man touched the brim of his dusty hat. "Afternoon. Heard we had a new doc in town. Thought I'd ride up and welcome ya."

Martin set his box on the worn porch planks and approached the fence to extend his hand. "That's mighty kind of you. I'm Martin Lancaster." He looked into the man's deeply tanned face, taking in the lines at the corners of his eyes, the two days' growth of dark beard shot with gray, the eyes so blue it was like peering into the sky. He pegged his visitor to be in his late thirties, perhaps early forties.

"Good to meet ya, Dr. Lancaster. Name's Dalton Pringle. I'm sheriff in these parts." Dalton's palm was warm and his grip strong as he shook Martin's hand. "We been in need of a doctor 'round here for some time now."

"Yes, I heard that when I was in my last year of residency and decided to come west." Martin looked out over the land. "It's beautiful here."

Dalton turned to take in the view as if just noticing it. "Yup, that it is. But dangerous, too, if you don't know how to treat her." He looked down at Martin. "Do you have all you need? Supplies, that kind of thing?"

Martin gestured toward the hill. "I was going to make a trip into town after I finished a few more things. Is the general store still open?"

Dalton nodded as his horse shifted beneath him and he reached down to pat the animal's neck. "Easy, girl. You're okay." He tilted his head toward the clear, endless sky. "She's been edgy all day. We might be in for a bit of a blow tonight."

Martin looked up too. "Really? Well, I'm no veterinarian, so I'll have to trust you on that."

Dalton grinned, and Martin felt a rush in his groin just like he used to feel when he had spent time with Professor Albright back in school. It was just as confusing now as it had been then. He dropped his gaze, squinting as he looked toward town. "Who's the storekeeper?"

"Cooper Pritchett. He's a good man, shrewd but honest. You'll want to introduce yourself and make a good impression because all post goes through him, too." He touched the brim of his hat and nodded. "I'd best be moving on. Have to check out some tell of men stealing cattle on the outskirts."

"All right then, Sheriff. It was kind of you to stop by."

"I reckon we'll be seeing each other pretty regular," Dalton said, and held his eyes a moment longer than necessary. "You take care, Doc." He tugged the reins to turn his horse, and Martin stood watching him ride off, the sheriff's broad shoulders eclipsing, for a moment, the sun.

The frantic knock came later that evening as Martin was unpacking what he promised himself was the last box of the night. He hurried to open the door, shushing Biscuit, who followed barking at his heels. Cooper Pritchett, the storekeeper, stood on the porch, his face pale and the wisps of silver hair atop his head dancing in the gusting wind. Pritchett staggered through the door carrying one end of a makeshift stretcher on which lay the sheriff, his face, so tanned and healthy that afternoon, now gray and hollow.

"Dear God, what happened?" Martin asked as the storekeeper's gangly young son followed his father through the door, struggling to hold up the other end of the stretcher.

"Been shot," Pritchett gasped. "In the chest. Surprised some cattle rustlers outside of town."

"Back here," Martin directed, leading them through the house to the room where he had begun to set up his operatory. "Lay him on the table. That's it. Mind his head now. Good, good."

Martin got to work, unbuttoning the bloody denim shirt to reveal a layer of soft, black chest hair. On the sheriff's left breast Martin found a gaping red hole where the bullet had entered the man's flesh. "He's still alive. Must have missed his heart," he said, turning to Pritchett. "Have you had any medical training?" The storekeeper's eyes widened, and he shook his head. "Well, you're about to. You," Martin pointed to Pritchett's son, "what's your name?"

The boy swallowed hard, his face pale. "David, sir."

"Good. David, take these towels here and heat some water in the kitchen. I want it boiling. Put the towels in the basin in there and pour the water over them. Then bring me three of them that have been wrung out. Got it?"

David nodded, grabbed an armload of clean white towels, and darted from the room. Martin poured fresh water from a pitcher into a basin and quickly scrubbed his hands, all the while snapping instructions to the storekeeper. Pritchett jumped as if he had been branded then came to life and began to hustle about the room. He grabbed instruments Martin described to him and helped clamp off the severed arteries. The bullet had narrowly missed Dalton's heart, ricocheting off two of his ribs before lodging itself in a third.

Martin and Pritchett worked on the sheriff for hours as word of the shooting spread through town. Dalton's deputy came to pace in Martin's living room, hat in hand, sitting now and then to take solace in Biscuit's attentions as the storm outside bore down. With a morbid sense of curiosity, neighbors and friends waited outside the doctor's house, debating who would take over Dalton's duties should he die—certainly not his deputy, who couldn't hit the side of a building with a gun full of buckshot.

Several hours after the falling rains had chased away the townsfolk, Martin put in the final stitch to close the wound in Dalton's chest. The sheriff's breathing sounded better and his color had returned. While Pritchett was in the kitchen helping his son sterilize the instruments, Martin ran his gaze over Dalton's body. His hairy chest was broad and firm. His nipples, brown and small, stood hard and tall in the cool night air. The man still wore his undergarment, but his legs were well-muscled and tan, covered with the same black hair as his chest, the sight of which made a warm ache bloom in Martin's own chest.

Resisting the impulse to fully undress the sheriff, Martin covered him with two sheets and took the pocked and bloody bullet with him as he crept from the room. His eyes burned with exhaustion, and his back ached from the hours he'd spent leaning over the table.

He helped Pritchett and his son clean up then saw them to the door, thanking them for their help and assuring the storekeeper that Dalton was resting comfortably.

Martin cleaned the bullet and placed it in a crystal dish beside his bed. He slept fitfully that night, tossing and turning, getting up now and then to check on the sheriff, his first real patient. Finally, exasperated, he wrapped a blanket around his shoulders and sat in a chair in the back room. Dalton's steady breathing soon lulled him to sleep, and he passed the night beside the sheriff.

Early the next morning, Martin came awake to find Dalton staring at him, and he jumped from his chair.

"How bad is it, Doc?" Dalton's voice was raspy.

Martin helped him take a few sips of water. "You were shot in the chest, left side. The bullet bounced off two ribs and stuck in a third. Nearly hit your heart."

Dalton closed his eyes. "Wouldn't matter. I got a tough heart." And he fell asleep again.

Dalton spent several days in the doctor's care, during which time Martin found his home inundated by single women from town. They came to call with homemade food to help the sheriff get his strength back. Martin grew weary of these intrusions but managed to keep his manner polite as the women appeared at his door, giggling and flirtatious, carrying pots of stew and baskets of bread. Dalton received the women cordially but with a cool detachment that provided them little encouragement.

At night, when it was just the two of them, Martin and Dalton talked over the hearty meals prepared by the women in town. Martin felt the difference in their ages and backgrounds fade away, and he came to know Dalton as a man, not just his patient or the town sheriff.

"Ever been married?" Martin asked Dalton one night, his back to him as he ladled stew into a bowl.

"Came close once," he replied. "But the fever took her eight years ago."

"Oh, I'm sorry," Martin said over his shoulder.

Dalton nodded. "How 'bout you?"

"No, never." He picked up the sheriff's empty bowl and re-filled it. "Ever thought about trying again?"

Dalton squinted at him. "What's on your mind, Doc?"

Martin set the bowl before him. "Just making conversation."

Dalton paused to take a bite of stew. "I'm forty-three years ancient, never been married, and only been serious with one gal." He shrugged then winced at the pull on his stitches. "Guess I'm an old prairie bachelor at heart." He looked up. "How old are you, if you don't mind my asking?"

"I don't mind. Twenty-seven."

Dalton grinned and shook his head. "Whole lotta rowdiness still burnin' in you."

Martin felt his cheeks flush. "Well, I've always been told I'm mature for my age, so I don't think there's much rowdiness left. I'm of a different constitution than most men you might be familiar with."

Dalton looked at him so long and intently Martin finally shifted in his seat and said, "What?" more defensively than he had intended.

The sheriff nodded slowly, his eyes never leaving Martin's face. "I was thinking you might be right about that, Doc. You're not like the men I'm familiar with."

Martin, flustered at the direction the conversation was taking, started asking about the wound in Dalton's chest. A quiet, sexy smile crossed the sheriff's face, a smile that wrapped a tight fist around Martin's heart and made his cock suddenly grow hard. To cool his blood he thought about the town preacher's wife, a homely woman named Gerta who excelled at pie-baking.

"The wound's all right," Dalton answered. "You saved my life. I won't forget that."

Martin shrugged. "It's why I came here."

"To save my life?" Dalton asked, and Martin felt himself blush again.

Later that night, Martin helped the sheriff into the spare bed he'd set up in a second bedroom. As Dalton eased himself beneath the covers, Martin couldn't help noticing the long, firm outline of the man's erection beneath his undergarment. His breath caught in his throat, and like the answering cry of a coyote on the plains, his own cock roared to full-blown life.

"Do you have everything you require?" Martin's voice caught as he tried to look anywhere but at Dalton's "condition."

The sheriff gave him an assessing look. "For now."

Martin nodded once and fled to the door, looking over his shoulder to say, "Have a good rest then."

"Yup. You do the same, Doc."

The sheriff left Martin's house in a week's time, well on his way to full recovery. The men who'd shot him hadn't been caught, and town gossip had it they'd fled south. Each night after he got into bed, Martin held the bullet he had pulled from Dalton's chest. He felt its rough texture and the partially flattened side where it had lodged so close to Dalton's heart. During these moments he felt an odd envy of the thing for accomplishing what Martin himself finally admitted he wanted to do himself.

One bright October afternoon as Martin fixed his fence, he turned at the sound of hooves to find Dalton riding up. The sheriff dismounted and pushed through the gate, wincing at the squeal of the hinges.

"Needs oil," Dalton said.

Martin blew out a breath and nodded. "Sure does. A lot of things around here need my attention, but I haven't had time, what with half the town being sick."

Dalton grinned and kicked at the dirt. "Yup, I heard about that. Thought you should know Mabel Holcombe might have undercooked the stew she served at the church social."

Martin and Dalton looked at each other for a moment then laughed themselves silly.

"That woman will be the death of this entire town one day," Martin said. "Someone has to tell her she *cannot* cook."

"Not if that someone values his life." Dalton looked around Martin's property. "You sure need help up here. How 'bout I pitch in as payback for putting me right again?"

Martin had always considered himself independent to a fault, but he surprised himself by accepting Dalton's offer. Over the next two weeks, Dalton spent his free time working with Martin on his property, and by the first of November the doctor's house was ready for the coming winter. That final evening, Martin laid a fire in the stone fireplace and poured a glass of whiskey for the man he now considered his friend. When his thoughts wandered to romantic longings, he stubbornly reined them back. He didn't want to ruin a good friendship like he'd done with Professor Albright.

Dalton came through the door and shivered as he kicked off his muddy boots. "Going to be snow before the week is out," he muttered. He found the drink waiting by his chair and downed it in a gulp, closing his eyes as the warmth spread through his body. "Thanks. I needed that."

Martin poured him another whiskey, then a glass for himself. They sat before the fire, Biscuit lying between them, and talked of the approaching holidays.

"I usually get stuck spending Christmas in jail watching the convicts," Dalton grumbled. "Been years since I've known anyone I wanted to spend that much time with."

Martin nodded thoughtfully and sipped his whiskey. "I've

always lived close to my parents, so I've always spent the holidays with them. This'll be the first season I'll be alone."

Dalton watched him from the corner of his eye. "No one in town you want to be with?"

Martin shrugged. "No one. Why?"

"Not even Mary Westford?"

Martin's eyes widened as Dalton roared with laughter. "You're serious? Mary Westford? No, no, I don't think so."

"I know for a fact she'd like to find you under her tree this year," Dalton teased through his laughter. "She's hung mistletoe on every doorframe in town hoping to trap you into a kiss."

"You can't be serious!"

"I am." Dalton grinned mischievously.

"You're a damned liar."

"Swear on the bullet you pulled out of my chest."

Martin's mind conjured images of himself masturbating furiously while clutching the bullet, and he fell silent. Looking away from Dalton's hot blue gaze, he took a swallow of his drink and fought to keep his sudden erection at bay.

Dalton suggested a game of poker, but Martin shook his head. "I don't have any money for cards, especially with the likes of you, Dalton Pringle."

"You're not suggesting I cheat, are you?" Dalton growled. "That's akin to slander in these parts."

"Fine, I take it back."

"Too late, you already said it. And to make up for it, you have to play."

Martin sighed but relented, and Dalton suggested they play for articles of clothing, which he agreed to. It wasn't until he had lost his first hand and gotten up to fetch a sock from his bureau that he realized his folly. Through his laughter, Dalton explained that when Martin lost, he was to shed an article of clothing he was currently wearing, not pull one from his chest of drawers. Martin refused until Dalton pointed out that he had already agreed to the conditions of the game, and so he reluctantly pulled a sock off his foot.

Several hands and several drinks later, both men sat barechested and barefoot before the fire as the wind howled outside. Martin was down to his undergarment, and his head felt fuzzy with whiskey. Across the table, Dalton was down to his jeans but seemed unaffected by the liquor. Several times Martin caught Dalton's eyes roving to the young doctor's chest and he took the opportunity to inspect the sheriff's body as well. The scar over the man's heart was beginning to fade, though the black hair around it had turned white. Pretending to examine the cards in his hand, Martin lowered his gaze to see how his own body looked. The weeks of physical labor around his small homestead had firmed his muscles. His nipples, the size of half dollars and pink, stood up firm beneath the light brown hair that covered his torso. His cock, hard for more than an hour now, strained against the confines of his undergarment. He had the taste of copper in his mouth.

Looking up, Martin caught Dalton barely hiding a smile as he surveyed his cards. Martin forced himself to focus on his own hand and studied it with dread: he held absolutely nothing of worth. Martin swallowed and peered up at Dalton, who raised an eyebrow.

"Want any cards?" Dalton asked.

"Yes, please. Four."

"Four? My, my, my, you must have a solid hand."

Martin inspected his four new cards and felt his gut clench. They were even worse than the ones he'd had. He would lose his last article of clothing, and Dalton would see his erection and know him for what he was: a sodomite.

"Dealer takes one." Grinning, Dalton dealt himself a card then looked up at Martin. "Ready?"

Martin sighed. "Ready." He laid down his hand, and Dalton laughed as he showed Martin his full house.

"Well, I guess that would mean I win." Dalton sat back in his chair, his hands clasped over his lap. "And you, my good doctor, lose your drawers."

Martin sat back and crossed his arms. "I protest. This was a setup."

Dalton shrugged. "I don't cheat at cards. I'm the law in this town. How would that look?" He lifted his chin at Martin. "Shuck 'em."

Defeated, Martin got to his feet, hesitated a moment, then slid his undergarment down his legs. He looked into the fire as he stood before Dalton, his cock hard and throbbing.

Dalton's voice was low and husky. "You got some cock on you, Doc."

Martin mustered his courage and gazed at Dalton, suddenly caught in the man's dangerous stare. The sheriff licked his lips and pressed the palm of his hand against his own bulging crotch.

"I..." Martin began but was cut off by a pounding on the door and a girl's high-pitched squeal.

"Dr. Lancaster! Dr. Lancaster!"

Martin quickly pulled on his undergarment and trousers then struggled into his shirt as he headed for the door. Dalton gathered his clothes and ducked into the nearest hiding place, Martin's bedroom.

The doctor opened the door to admit a pale young girl with auburn hair and a population of freckles on her face. He grasped her gently by the shoulders.

"What's wrong?"

"It's my mama," the girl gasped. "She's havin' a baby, but it ain't goin' well. The midwife sent me to fetch you."

Martin's head cleared immediately, the fuzziness of the whiskey gone as adrenaline burned through him. He sat the girl by the fire to warm her up and dashed into his operatory to grab his bag. Stepping into his bedroom, he found Dalton on the edge of his bed, shirt still off, the bullet Martin kept by his bed held in the palm of his hand.

"I have to go." Martin tucked in his shirt and pulled on his jacket. "A birth isn't going right." He paused and looked at Dalton. "Are you...?"

Dalton stared up at him, his eyes calm. "You keep this by your bed?"

Martin nodded, his stomach knotting like snakes.

"I always wondered what you did with it."

"You were my first patient," Martin tried to explain. There was more to it, so much more, but no time to divulge his reasoning and feelings. "I'm sorry. I need to go."

"I know. Go. Save a life."

Martin moved into the living room and helped the girl tie her coat more tightly against the wind. They stepped into the cold night, and he loaded her into his wagon then headed down the frozen, rutted road.

Later that night, beneath the white gaze of the waning moon, Martin returned home. He unhitched his horse and led him to the stable, then staggered through the back door of his house and scrubbed up in the operatory. He was tired, and a cold seed of worry had begun to unfurl in his gut now that the medical emergency was done with. He worried about Dalton and how their card game and the sheriff's discovery of the bullet might affect their friendship.

Drying his hands, Martin made his way into the parlor to

find that the fire had died. He gathered some smaller bits of wood for the stove in his bedroom and, carrying a lamp, made his way through the house with Biscuit trailing.

His bedroom was cold and dark, and his mind was distracted with thoughts of Dalton as he arranged the firewood so it would catch easily. Once he had the fire lit he started to undress.

"Did you save her?"

Martin jumped and let out a shout, turning to find Dalton lying in his bed. The sheets were down to the middle of his chest, exposing his bare skin.

"You scared five years off my life," Martin said.

"Well, now we're a little closer in age." Dalton sat up against the headboard, and the sheet fell to his waist. "Did you save her?"

"What?" Martin forced his gaze up from the man's bare torso to his blue eyes reflecting firelight. "Um, yes, I did. The baby was breach. I had to turn it. But I saved them both."

"Was it Polly Olmsted?"

"Yes."

"Boy or girl?"

"Boy."

"They've been wanting a boy," Dalton said. "Polly and Jack have got themselves four girls and now a boy."

"They were very grateful." Martin took a few steps forward. "I don't know why you're in my bed, but—"

"Yes, you do." Dalton reached over and pulled back the sheets on the other side of the bed. "We've been dancing around this for a while now. It's high time we both admitted it."

Martin hesitated a moment, then stripped off his clothes and slid in beside Dalton. The man's body had warmed the sheets, and Martin sighed as the sheriff pulled him against his hard, strong form.

Their mouths collided, tongues bursting past their lips, the passion that had been building from the first day they met finally finding release. Dalton's beard scratched along Martin's face and lips, and his powerful, calloused hands moved down Martin's body to clutch his erection.

"Oh, God," Martin gasped. No man had ever touched him in this way.

Dalton slid beneath the sheets, his mouth and tongue tasting Martin's body. He paused to suck hard on Martin's nipples, and the doctor groaned, pressing his hands against the back of Dalton's head. The scratch of the sheriff's beard brought up gooseflesh on Martin's arms, and he tilted back his head, closing his eyes against the rush of sensation.

Moving lower, Dalton came to Martin's cock and ran his tongue along its length. The doctor groaned and squirmed, but Dalton used the weight of his body to pin Martin in place, then took his cock in his throat. He sucked him slow and deep, the fingers of one hand curled tight around the base of the shaft while in the other he held Martin's balls. They were smaller than Dalton's but fit just fine in the palm of his hand. The doctor's cock was circumcised, and Dalton sucked hard on the bulbous tip.

After a time, Dalton released Martin's cock and slid up the man's body, poking his head from beneath the sheets to draw in a deep breath of cool air. They kissed again, slower and deeper this time, tongues twisting like rope. Martin's hand grazed the scar over Dalton's chest, and the doctor pulled away, his brow furrowed.

"I'm sorry. Did that hurt?" Martin asked.

"No," Dalton said, and kissed him again. "My old heart's full of scars. I'm surprised you found a way inside."

At these words, Martin felt a jolt race through him and rolled

Dalton onto his back. He lowered himself along the man's body, pausing for a time to suck the small, hard points of his nipples. He ran his tongue through Dalton's dark chest hair to his navel, slipping the tip of his tongue into the deep, swirled cavern.

The head of the sheriff's cock pulsed and throbbed beneath Martin's jaw, commanding his attention, and he finally addressed it. Dalton's cock was long and thick, uncut and meaty. Martin peeled back the foreskin and pursed his lips around the shiny, wet glans. He had never touched another man like this, and the salty taste of Dalton's cock burst in his mouth like ripe fruit. Suddenly he couldn't get enough, and he filled his mouth with Dalton's cock. The blunt tip bumped and skidded along the roof of his mouth, poking into the back of his throat and causing him to gag.

"Easy, Doc," Dalton said. He pulled the sheets back so Martin could take a gulp of fresh air. "Have you ever done this before?"

Martin shook his head, coughing as his eyes watered.

Dalton laid a hand along his face and smiled. "I've only been with two other men, both for just a night and rougher than a stampede." He pulled Martin's face close and kissed his forehead. "Nothing like this."

Easing Martin onto his back, Dalton knelt between his legs and eased them up to his shoulders. He lowered his face into the crack of Martin's ass and flicked his tongue across the tight, puckered anus.

"Oh, God," Martin breathed. "What are you doing?"

"Relax," Dalton told him. "Trust me." He pressed his mouth against Martin's hole and slid his tongue deep into the man. Martin groaned and clutched the sheets beneath him as Dalton did things to him he had never imagined.

Just when Martin thought he couldn't take any more, Dalton

raised his head and slipped a finger inside him. He felt the invading finger like a punch in the gut and lifted his head from the pillow to stare at Dalton's face illuminated by the lamplight.

Dalton raised his eyebrows. "Want a little more?"

Martin nodded then dropped his head back. The second finger slipped inside, and he groaned again as his cock jumped, slapping audibly against his belly.

"Feel okay?" Dalton asked.

Martin had no voice, so he raised his head and nodded. Dalton's fingers drove in and pulled out of him faster and faster, and just when Martin thought he would lose control, they stopped and withdrew. Dalton adjusted his position and Martin looked down to see him spit into his open palm. Dalton reached down to spread his spit on something out of Martin's sightline, then moved closer to him.

Suddenly Martin felt as if he were being split open. The fat, round head of Dalton's cock pushed into him, and Martin let out a cry that startled Biscuit into a volley of barks. Dalton snapped at Biscuit to keep quiet, and the dog lay down again by the stove as the sheriff turned his attention back to Martin. Slowly, so slowly, Dalton eased deeper into him, his cock parting muscles until finally he knelt fully inside him.

"Oh, my God." Martin sighed and raised his head just as Dalton lowered his to press a kiss to his lips. "Oh, my God. This is amazing."

"Feels all right?" Dalton asked.

"It feels very right."

Dalton withdrew then entered him again, a little faster this time. He pulled out and pushed in again, then again, faster until his hips found a rhythm and he drove into his lover with a rugged power that shook the bedstead. Martin groaned and thrashed as Dalton's cock pumped into him, invading him, opening him up.

The familiar tingle of orgasm started in his prostate, and Martin reached down to grab hold of his cock, stroking himself to a powerful climax. The hot, thick semen splattered along his torso, mixing with his and Dalton's sweat and leaving him sticky and exhausted.

Dalton thrust into him a few more times then screwed up his face as he let loose his own load deep inside Martin. He collapsed on top of him, his sweaty body coated with Martin's semen. They kissed for a time, Dalton's softening cock still held tight in Martin's ass.

Finally, Dalton eased himself out of Martin and stood to collect their undergarments, which they used to clean themselves up. He added wood to the fire, patted Biscuit's head, then joined Martin in bed again, giving him a gentle, lingering kiss. They fell asleep in minutes, Martin's arm slung across Dalton's chest, his fingers resting against the man's scar.

As the wind whips snow harder against Martin's house, he gets up to place another log on the fire. In the corner stands a Christmas tree, one he and Dalton had ridden out into the woods for and cut down together two mornings ago. Martin had started a snowball fight, which ended in a long, deep kiss once he had been tackled by Dalton as he attempted to flee the sheriff's better aim through the drifting snow.

They had put up the tree that afternoon, decorating it with tinsel and paper ornaments, talking about their childhoods and Christmases past. Dalton had confessed he hadn't had a Christmas tree since leaving his family's ranch, and Martin had asked him to put the tin star Martin's father had made for him on top.

Martin looks forward to Dalton's arrival later tonight, like he once did that jolly burglar Saint Nick. The sheriff will come in the back door and find Martin waiting nude in bed, and they'll make Christmas memories of their own.

The wind pushes against the glass again, and Martin refills his sherry, then takes it to the window where he stands and looks out at the town. His eye is drawn to the glow of lamplight in the window of the sheriff's office just visible through the snowfall, and he feels the first pulse of arousal as he thinks about the long, hard gift Dalton will be bringing him later.

MIND IN THE MIDDLE

Julia Talbot

You reckon Tyler will take it all this year?" some old fart was saying, not knowing Tyler Anderson was walking right by him, separated only by the wall of galvanized steel tubing and Skoal advertising banners.

"Not if he don't get his head out of his ass," geezer number two muttered. "You see him go down in the well today?"

"Yep. Didn't even make three seconds."

Cheeks on fire, Tyler kept walking, heading up the long walk of shame to the locker rooms where he could get out of his chaps and vest. He was limping a little from where that goddamned Brahma had stomped his shit but good.

Get his head out of his ass. Tyler snorted. No, it wasn't just that he'd torn a tendon in his arm a month back, or that he'd drawn one of the biggest, strongest bulls on the circuit. Not a bit. That was the hazard of being on top of the bull-riding game. Everyone speculated when you had a few bad rides, from the

Pro Rodeo News reporters to the gate-pullers on the ground. He'd just hit a slump, was all, and while Tyler wasn't one to hold anyone else responsible for his problems, he laid the blame for this dry spell firmly at Sevi Rosa's doorstep.

Damn that beautiful Brazilian bastard, dumping him the first week of finals in Las Vegas. What a shitty thing to do.

The after-party was already going strong in the hotel ballroom when Tyler got there, stopping to sign autographs on the way in. Wouldn't you know it, the minute he headed to the bar to get a Jack and Coke, there was Sevi, chatting up some girl with tousled blonde hair and a tiny pink tank top.

"Hey, Tyler," his buddy Craig hollered, waving at him from a table. "Come on over."

Tearing his eyes away from Sevi's sleek, compact body and pretty eyes, Tyler nodded and headed to his friend, grinning a little. Craig bounced along to the music, which was by some band Tyler didn't know, looking like he wanted to two-step someone right into the ground.

"Hey, Ty. You rode like you were somewhere else tonight," Craig said, blue eyes twinkling, blond hair flopping in his face.

Tyler sighed. "Maybe I was somewhere else, at least in my head."

"Yeah, in the sack with Rosa. Man, you gotta give that up."

"I did." Tyler sipped his drink and looked around to make sure no one heard that. Hell, half the riders knew anyway. You didn't spend ten months out of twelve on the road with the same hundred guys and not have them know, but it just wasn't something you wanted to advertise. "Or at least he gave me up."

"So get your head past it. Hey, honey," Craig said to a pretty brunette wearing too much eyeliner. "Wanna dance?"

Tyler was alone again, as Craig took off with the girl, whirling her into a quickstep. He sucked back the rest of his drink, pondering whether he should get another or start on some Bud Light. Shit, maybe he ought to just give up and head back to the hotel room, ice up his arm, and sleep off his angry.

"Hey, cowboy. Can a guy sit with you?" The voice belonged to Andy West, a cowboy Tyler didn't know well. Tyler looked up to the man a little, and that made it hard to be coherent when he was around. Lord knew Tyler was hoping he lasted into his mid thirties like Andy had, winning two national championships in eight years. Didn't hurt that Andy was pretty to look at, with thick, close-cropped dark hair and light-light gray eyes.

Nodding at the seat across from him, Tyler waved a little. "Sure, man. Have a sit."

Folding long-assed legs up, Andy sat and handed him a long-neck beer. "Here. You look like you could use it."

"Thanks." Shit, he hated to be that obvious. Not knowing what else to say, Tyler just sat there picking at the label on the bottle.

Andy didn't say nothing either, at least until Tyler looked up for the third or fourth time and found Sevi Rosa across the room. Then Andy said, "Don't."

"Don't what?" Tyler returned, eyebrows rising up and up.

Sitting back, boots crossed at the ankles, Andy pulled a pack of smokes out of a shirt pocket and offered Tyler one. He shook his head. Andy lit up, blowing a stream of smoke out before he answered, voice so low the music almost covered it.

"Don't let Rosa twist you up and ruin your run this year. He's a shit."

Hot anger roared in Tyler's brain for all of a minute, and he actually rose halfway out of his chair before the ass-kicking urge backed off and the truth of it sank in. Sevi was a shit, no two ways about it.

"Yeah, I know. Doesn't make it easier."

"Well, maybe this will. He pulls this crap every year going into the finals. Trying to slow down the leader."

"Yeah?" Well, that felt like a boot to the gut. Or maybe a hoof. "It work for him often?"

"So far he's two for five." Andy gave him a long look as the cigarette got stubbed out, impossible to misread.

Tyler's fingers stilled on the beer bottle. "You?"

"Yeah. Three years ago." He got a grin, wry as anything. "I was fool enough to fall for it."

"Shit. Why didn't anyone tell me?"

"Aw, hell, cowboy." Andy lit another cigarette, and this time Tyler took one when he offered. "You think Chris Packard or either of the Garza boys are going to admit Sevi came on to them? And then there's me. You don't know me from Adam's housecat. Would you have believed me?"

"Probably not." Tyler could be a stubborn cuss when he had a mind to be. He knew he was a damned fool. Suddenly the crowd and the loud band were too much for him, and he hopped up, saying, " 'Scuse me."

The little hotel ballroom seemed so close, so full of people as he blundered toward the door. His hands clenched to fists as Sevi Rosa looked over and gave him a cocky grin, and Tyler's boots turned that direction without a single thought. He would have marched right over, too, and popped Sevi one, but Andy caught his arm and steered him away.

"You go after him here you'll get bumped off the circuit," he said, shoving Tyler into the hallway, where at least he could breathe.

"You're right. Sorry. I just..."

Andy looked at him a minute, cigarette still smoldering. "You wanna go get a real drink? I've already cracked the minibar thing in my room." There was something in Andy's look, something in the invitation...Yeah. Okay. Yeah. This might be the best cure for a breakup after all.

"Sure. Why not?"

The smile Andy gave him left him blinking, it was so bright and hot. Something south of his big belt buckle shifted, rose a little. Good to know he wasn't dead after all. Tyler trailed after Andy, watching that tiny cowboy ass as it moved, smiling a little. Sevi might be prettier than Andy in the face, but ass-wise Andy was the clear-cut winner.

Oh, if Sevi could see him now. That thought kept him going all the way up the stairs to the third floor, where Andy swiped a card in the door of room 335 and let them inside. The place was neat as a pin, no sign the guy even lived there save a bag on the luggage rack and an old army rucksack.

"This is unnatural, man," Tyler said, looking around.

"What?" Andy gave him a sheepish look. "I tend to lose things if I don't keep them packed up. You want that drink?"

"No." Tyler took off his hat and let it sail to the bed Andy hadn't been sleeping in. "I want something else."

"You sure?"

Stepping right up to Andy, Tyler put one hand on the man's chest and nodded. "I'm sure."

"Well, come on and get it then."

The first kiss was awkward as hell, neither of them willing to give an inch as they came together—Andy's hand cupping the back of Tyler's head, Tyler's mouth mashed under Andy's. If he'd wondered whether this was another suave seduction, another bid like Sevi's, the thought was put to rest by that meeting of lips.

One long thigh slid between his, pushing up, and that was that. Tyler wrapped around Andy and clung, kissing like there was no tomorrow, his cock hard as a rock. They humped a little, hands moving, kissing until they couldn't breathe. Then Andy pushed him back and tore at his shirt.

Shirts, Wranglers, boots—they all went flying, his and Andy's. Before Tyler knew it they were both naked, both checking each other out. Andy had a farmer's tan, everything pale but his arms and neck, and right above one nipple sat a huge scar, one Tyler remembered Andy getting a couple years back when he went ass over teakettle and landed on the horns instead of between them.

Andy jumped a little under Tyler's touch, and Tyler grinned, pinching that nipple a little as it rose hard beneath his hand. That got him more than a jump—it got him a moan. Andy's cock twitched against his belly.

"Like that, huh?"

"Yeah. You might could tell."

"Uh-huh." As the other nipple got the same treatment, Tyler was fascinated with the flush that rose under Andy's skin. Sevi hadn't been able to stand Tyler touching him there. Sevi was all about the cock, really. 'Course, thinking about what an idiot he'd been with Sevi might just ruin the mood. "What else do you like?" Tyler asked, just to get his head going in a different direction.

"I like it all, honey," Andy replied, pushing him back until his knees hit the bed. "I like it here." Those long, scarred fingers slipped across his throat, down his chest. "And here," he said, trailing a hand down his belly, pulling at the little line of hair there.

"And here?" Tyler asked, pushing that hand down to his cock, his eyes closing as Andy's fingers wrapped around him. Fuck yeah.

"That's the best part, honey."

Tyler's eyes flew open again when he felt Andy's mouth on his cock, hot and wet, sliding from tip to base and back again. Rough and firm, Andy's tongue stroked along the underside, along the big vein. Then those hot lips closed right over the tip of his cock, sinking down, and Tyler just moaned, his body twisting on the sheets. How long had it been since someone else had done the doing? Sevi wouldn't suck on a dare.

God.

Tyler let himself go when Andy cupped his ass in those big hands and made encouraging noises. He let his hips hump up and fuck Andy's face, let his orgasm rise along his spine, ready to unload any second.

Which was when Andy stopped, of course.

Rising up on his elbows, Tyler blinked, his muscles shuddering under his skin. The smell of them made him fucking drool, all hot musk and sweat. "What the fuck, man?" he asked, his voice sounding like sandpaper on a block of wood.

"Want you to fuck me, Tyler. Don't want to waste it."

Oh, Jesus. His belly went tight as a board, his cock jerking madly even as Andy's spit dried on it. He nodded wildly.

"Yeah, yeah. Okay. I don't have...do you?"

"Uh-huh." There was that damned grin again, putting the weirdest feeling in Tyler's belly. Andy went on, "I was hoping."

"Then bring it on, buddy." He'd bet Andy's ass was tight, hot, too damned good to be true.

Andy left him for a moment, coming back with condoms and a tube of lube, the man making a helluva picture, all lean muscle and hard cock standing up against his belly. Damn.

He had to touch. Had to. Tyler reached out and slid his hand along the underside of that long cock, grasping it and giving it a few good tugs.

"Nice, buddy."

"Fuck," Andy said, swaying a little. "You want me to last, you oughta let go."

Despite this being the hottest, smoothest skin Tyler had ever felt, he let go. He wanted to fuck Andy like there was no tomorrow, and he wanted that cowboy to be with him all the way.

"Come on, Andy. Wanna," Tyler said, holding out his hand, still damp from the hot drops of Andy's precum.

"How do you want me?" Andy asked, taking his hand and kneeling next to his hip.

If it were Sevi, well, Tyler would put the man on his hands and knees and fuck him into the middle of next week to pay for what he'd done. Andy, though, Andy he wanted to see. Wanted to look him right in the eye.

"On your back, buddy."

God. Andy rolled right to his back, drawing his knees up to his chest. Just watching made Tyler think he might explode, but he had to get in there, had to feel, so he took the lube and got his fingers wet, shoving two of them right into Andy's body, stretching that little hole almost impossibly.

"Fuck!" Andy arched, body rolling up, then down, tight and hot around his fingers. Then the muscles he'd breached relaxed, letting him in.

"Oh, I need that. Can I, buddy?"

"Come on, come on, come on," Andy chanted, rolling, rippling for him.

The condom fought him at every fucking step, but Tyler got it on, got himself all slicked up and slid between Andy's spread legs, pushing right into that sweet cowboy ass, just like he was meant to, his head falling forward as he groaned. It was just like he'd known it would be, so hot and tight Tyler thought he was going to go off like the Fourth of July.

Andy panted beneath him, chest and face flushed, cock straining.

If he could have, Tyler would have reached for Andy's cock, would have stroked the man off like crazy. He couldn't let go of

Andy's hips, though, squeezing hard enough to bruise. He rode Tyler like he would a bull, all focus and determination.

Finally it was Andy who got a hand free, reaching down to stroke himself, and the sight of it sent Tyler over, had him shooting like a bottle rocket, filling the condom with hot cum.

A few more strokes and Andy was right behind him, unloading gobs of cum all over their bellies and chests.

Tyler flopped down on Andy's chest, those long legs wrapping around him loosely as they relaxed. After a minute he pulled out, then tied off the condom to plop it into the trash can beside the bed. He glommed on to Andy and held on tight.

They dozed a bit, Andy stroking his back, light snores coming now and again, before it occurred to him.

"You won the championship three years ago, didn't you? I mean, I was a rookie that year, barely daring to get near you, but you didn't act like a guy who'd been jilted."

Andy chuckled, patting Tyler's ass. "Well, no. I didn't, did I? That's 'cause there was this new kid on the circuit, eager as a beaver, bright eyed and bushy tailed. He had the best ass I'd ever seen and I was way too busy falling for him to even worry on it."

"You mean...?" Tyler propped himself up, looking Andy in the eye. "Why didn't you say nothin'?"

"And have you kick my ass? I didn't know 'til I saw you with Sevi."

"Well, now you know." Tyler rested his chin on Andy's chest. "What are you gonna do about it?"

"For starters? Tell you to keep this," Andy squeezed Tyler's ass in both hands, "planted on that bull tomorrow. Got it?"

"Yeah. Yeah, buddy, I think I can do that."

The Sunday ride on the first weekend of finals was usually one to separate the men from the boys. Hell, most of them were hungover from the after-party, or tired out from traveling and shaking hands and shit.

Tyler Anderson was ready, though. He'd drawn a hell of a bull, he was set to ride, and he'd been able to look Sevi Rosa in the eye and smile, knowing somewhere back behind the chutes Andy West was rooting for him.

All he had to do was keep his mind in the middle.

That bull turned him every which way but loose, but Tyler stayed on. And as the eight-second buzzer went off, it was Andy he was thinking of, not Sevi Rosa.

Maybe he'd gotten his head out of his ass in time to take the whole game this year after all.

RANCH-HAND HOOKUP

Bearmuffin

The cowboys stopped dead in their tracks when Cody Barnes roared onto the Texas Star Ranch in his Chevy pickup. His incredible presence and powerful body dazzled them. Within seconds, each and every one of those hard-ridin' cocksuckers had a raging hard-on.

Cody's shaggy brown hair was hidden beneath a black Stetson. Heavy stubble peppered his rocky chin and square-jawed face. His neck was thick as a bull's, his shoulders massive and sturdy. Thick veins throbbed beneath his sweat-slicked slabs of muscle and smooth, golden-tanned skin.

The stud's beefy nipples stood stiff beneath a damp red button-up shirt, although a huge, gaping hole over his left pec exposed one of them, glowing with a single bead of hot sweat. The bottom of his shirt hung teasingly an inch above his navel.

One could glimpse his furrowed abs, which were covered in an expanse of brown swirling fur that disappeared behind his rawhide belt. Cody's tree-trunk thighs and juicy muscle butt bulged within his faded Wranglers. Tufts of sweaty pubic hair poked through a wide hole that had ripped open at his crotch, which had been worn through by his massive cockhead. His meaty, veiny cock snaked along the length of his inner thigh, held snug by faded denim. His bowling-ball biceps were awesome, but his bushy, sweat-dripping armpits made everyone drool. The cowboys surrounded Cody. The overpowering odor of raunchy manstud sailed up their noses and shot swift bolts of manlust to their pulsing groins.

Beau Ryan, owner of the Texas Star Ranch, fell in instant lust with Cody and offered him a job right there on the spot. The beefy stud equally mesmerized the rest of the cowboys, and he immediately became their pal. Nobody could have felt more welcome.

That first day, Cody put in twelve hours of rounding up, roping, and branding steers. At sunset, the other sweaty cowpunchers called it a day and headed for Hank's Bar. That's where a horny stud could swill down the coldest beer in town and watch pro football with some hard-workin', hard-drinkin' cowboys. Maybe he'd even find himself an accommodating ranch hand with a willing tongue and a tight asshole.

Cody headed to Beau's office to see how he'd done that day. Beau was mighty impressed with his new hired hand from Calgary, so he gave him a week's advance on his pay. The cowboy responded with a grateful grin. There was only one way to repay such generosity.

"I'm fucking horny," Cody husked. He unbuttoned his fly, and his lust-bloated cock rose up full mast in front of Beau's astonished eyes. Cody's shirt was tucked behind his belt, his jeans slung low over his lean hips. Beau's eyes were riveted to Cody's athletic, sweat-soaked body.

Cody smiled lewdly. He kissed Beau, who responded by running his hands all over Cody's chest. Cody felt the keen excitement he always experienced when a stud played with his muscles. He moaned, tongue-fucking Beau's mouth and swabbing spit as his boss played with his pecs.

Beau always thrilled to the touch of a manly cowboy's body. His blue eyes flashed with macho passion as his hands traveled across Cody's superb muscles. Beau unzipped his fly then pulled out his cock. He grabbed both their cocks and squeezed them hard. Now their cocks were jammed together.

Cody gasped when he felt Beau's powerful tool. He marveled at the strength pulsing within those big, throbbing blue veins. Beau glared at the precum drops oozing from their pissholes, dribbling down the full length of their cocks.

Beau played with Cody's nipples, gently tweaking them as Cody closed his eyes, threw back his head, and moaned his macho ecstasy and pleasure. "What a body," Beau muttered. "What a fucking hot body." Yeah. Beau was going to ride this hot cowboy. He was going to ram his cock up Cody's ass. He ran his tongue over the ranch hand's pecs. He loved how his body tasted—that raw, manly flavor of hot, ripe stud. He buried his face in one of Cody's armpits and inhaled deeply. The potent aroma made his cock swell and throb all the more.

Cody was more than pleased that Beau was admiring his body. And he was thrilled that Beau wanted him. His cock twitched and throbbed against Beau's spasming rod.

Beau turned Cody around, then stopped for a moment to admire the cowboy's powerful back. It was wide and tapered down to a narrow waist. Then his eyes took in Cody's spectacular ass: two bronzed globes of firm, muscular flesh. Beau rubbed his cock between Cody's sweaty asscheeks.

Cody shuddered when he felt his boss's fat cockhead against

his pucker. Beau smiled knowingly; this was the moment they both had been waiting for. At last he was going to fuck Cody's hot ass. Cody hunched down a bit so Beau could slip his cock inside his ass. He moaned pleasurably as his asshole gave way and allowed Beau's cock to slide easily into his hot, spasming hole. Beau shuddered at the incredible sensation of Cody's hot slick asshole sucking in his cock.

"Oh, yeah," Cody moaned. "Oh, yeah. Feels so good. So fucking good."

Beau hissed into Cody's ear, "Like my cock up your hole, huh?" Beau's hands were running all over Cody's arms. He squeezed the spectacular biceps and triceps. Cody pushed his hot, sweaty body against Beau, who slowly worked his cock up Cody's hole. Finally, Cody felt Beau's huge balls strike the base of his throbbing cock.

Cody cried out as he clamped his sphincter around the root of Beau's cock. "Fuck!" he exclaimed. "I love your fucking cock up my hole!"

Beau pumped Cody's butthole for a half-hour, fucking him doggie-style until they changed positions, with Cody now on the floor on his back. He thrust his legs over Beau's shoulders.

Cody's nipples were stiff, so Beau took one thick nipple into his mouth and bit it. "Yeeeeooow!" Cody yelled as he thrashed on the floor. Beau seesawed the edges of his teeth over the ultra-sensitive tip of Cody's nipple. The young stud jerked and moaned even more.

Beau bit into Cody's tits, sucking hard and long, taking one whole nipple into his mouth while tweaking the other. Cody's ass-hole clutched Beau's cock, and Cody was thrashing around like crazy. Beau's hot cock slid up and down inside Cody's twitching hole. "Awww, fuck! Aww, jeeez!" he screamed. Drops of hot precum oozed from Beau's huge cock, singeing Cody's asshole.

Finally, Beau knew he was ready to shoot his wad, so he drove his pelvis forward and rammed into Cody, who hunched down full force to meet Beau's powerful thrust. Cody smashed against Beau's groin.

"Yeeeeooow! Fuucckk! Yeaaahh!!!!" Beau screamed as he cleaved Cody's tight butt in two and hurtled thick loads of hot jizz into his throbbing butthole.

When Beau had shot the last of his hot wad, he pulled his cock from Cody's ass. Then he scuttled between Cody's thighs and swallowed the boy's cock to the root.

When Cody felt Beau's mouth engulf his entire shaft, he screamed. "Awwww! Fuucckk!! FUUUUCKK! I'M COMM-MINNNGG!" Cody pounded his fists against Beau's back. Beau rammed three fingers up Cody's cum-soaked asshole. The cowboy shuddered as he shot his load right into his boss's mouth. Beau swallowed as much cum as he could before it spilled out of his mouth and dribbled down his chin.

Afterward, Cody wiped his cum-drenched ass and cock with a hanky.

"You're one hell of a wild fuck," Beau told him.

Cody grinned. "You too."

They joined the other cowboys at Hank's Bar, where the men were rough, raw, and ready for action.

Once inside, they were met with a throng of black Stetsons and colorful button-up shirts. Cody ran into Ward Rogers, one of the horniest men on the ranch. He'd had his eye on Cody all day and was determined to fuck him. He was on his fourth beer. Ward started his usual shit, taunting Cody into a fight. He dared to call Cody a fag.

Well, even if he was new, Cody wasn't about to take shit from anyone, least of all Ward. The cowboys grinned knowingly. There was only one way to settle this.

"Take it out outside," the bartender said.

The sweaty crowd followed Cody and Ward to the parking lot. The men howled as the two cowboys stripped down and began to wrestle. The onlookers pulled out their cocks and jacked off as they watched, their lust-bloated rods oozing thick drops of precum. Hot jizz sputtered from their piss-slits and poured to the ground with a sizzling fizzle!

Ward tried to outmaneuver Cody, but the stud was lightning quick. Cody lunged at Ward, catching him fast in a face-crushing headlock.

Cody mashed Ward's craggy face into his raunchy armpit. The powerful stink rushed up Ward's nose. It excited him, made his cock quiver with lust. His cum-bloated balls danced inside his low-swinging nut sack.

"Yeah, fucker!" Cody hissed. "Ya like that fuckin' man-stink? Lap it up, stud! LICK MY PITS!"

Ward's licker came flying out of his mouth. He swirled it along Cody's sweaty armpit hairs, which scratched his face and wrapped around his fluttering tongue. Pungent blasts of hot man-stench scorched Ward's tongue, rushed up his dilated nostrils, and sent tears streaming down his sweaty face.

Cody held Ward fast in a bone-crushing belly-to-belly bear hug. Their cocks sputtered hard and long, thrusting upward, trapped between their sweat-drenched, muscled abs. Precum drooled from their piss slits, flowing in one long, sputtering drizzle to the pavement.

Cody forced his slobbering tongue between Ward's lips. Ward responded by thrusting his licker into the ranch hand's anxious mouth. The two fierce studs grunted and groaned, eagerly swapping hot macho spit with each other until it frothed and bubbled down the corners of their gasping mouths.

Ward bucked and yelped, but he was inexorably trapped in

Cody's powerful grip. Fisting their precum-dripping cocks, the cowboys roared with glee at Ward's predicament. Cody dug his thick, hairy fingers into the stud's sweaty haunches. He slapped the man's hot, slimy buttocks, then peeled them wide apart with his thumbs.

"YEEEAHH!" Cody howled fiercely, his savage face contorted with manly lust. "Gonna fuck ya, stud!" he growled. "Gonna fill your hot ass full of cock!" He hoisted Ward on top of his cock.

"NNNOOO! AWWWW! GODAMNNN! FUUUCK!" Ward screamed hoarsely when Cody rammed his meat all the way up his ass. The cowboys yowled like banshees as Cody fucked the living daylights out of Ward.

Ward wrapped his legs around Cody's waist, and Cody's burly arms flew around Ward's vein-corded bull neck. Ward brutally slammed his ass into Cody. The cowboy chewed on Ward's thick, sweat-soaked nipples and slobbered over his hard, sweaty pecs. Ward's eyes rolled back in their sockets and his drooling tongue flopped out of his mouth as his cock-hungry hole sucked around Cody's pile-driving cock. "AAAAAH, FUCK ME! FUCK ME, STUD!" he roared.

Some of the cowboys were already shooting their thick loads. Their piss-slits opened wide and out flew the thick blasts of jizz, splattering on Cody and Ward and drenching them both.

"Yeah, stud!" Cody grunted. "Unnngh, unnngh, unnngh!! I'm fuckin' your ass, buddy. I'm fuckin' your stinking ass but good!!!" Cody's huge boulder muscles rippled and bulged as his hairy butt heaved back and forth. He stud-slammed his thick eleven-inch tool in and out of Ward's sweat-dripping butthole. He shuddered, delirious with lust.

"Awwwww fuck!! Awwwww jeeez!!!" Cody cried. "GONNA SHOOT, STUD! GONNA FUCKIN' SHOOT!!!"

Cody's blazing eyes bulged, and his hot mouth gaped wide open. His slobbering tongue flopped out of his mouth as he power-slammed his dick of death up Ward's burning, aching butthole.

"Aaaaaaaargh!!!" Cody bellowed as he slammed forward one last time. He buried his cock to the root as his hairy, swinging balls smashed against Ward's. Big, scalding cum-spurts pumped up Ward's jizz-scorched hole. The burning juice sprayed from Cody's stud-nuts, filling Ward's ass. Ward squirmed, his powerful asshole squeezing the thick root of Cody's cock as it suctioned the hot cum from his bull-nuts.

"UNNGH! UNNNGH! AWWWWWWW FUCK! GOD-DAMN FUUUUCCCKKK!" Ward screamed. His cock swelled up and exploded, hurtling thick jets of semen between their bodies. The frothy hot cum sprayed out like a geyser, spewing all over the place. The cowboys cried lustily, shooting their huge loads over Cody and Ward and each other until every last one of them had emptied his hairy nuts and was drenched in a gushing sea of cum.

Cody soon found himself smack in the middle of a circle of savagely horny cowboys furiously pumping their thick, uncut, vein-pulsing pricks, their faces were contorted with lust. Their cocks suddenly rose full mast, dribbling thick streams of pre-cum.

"Wanna fuck?" they shouted.

"Fuck, yeah!" Cody howled. "Who's next?"

A WANTED MAN

Dale Chase

It wasn't my intention to become an outlaw, even though I was, in the spring of 1866, taken up by the Judson gang as they robbed the Mercantile Bank of Abilene, Kansas. Until then I was no more than a restless young man, having come of age on a local cattle ranch. Had I not been of a certain nature, I would've remained nothing more than one of the many who lost their money that fateful day. As it was, my life forever changed.

My monthly pay in hand, I had come to town to spend a goodly amount but not before depositing some of it at the bank. Dreams of one day going west led me to save my pay, and with each deposit San Francisco shone before me. As ranch life was steady and therefore of little excitement, I developed an interest in men famed for their gunplay and spent plenty of time discharging my weapon at small vermin and other targets about the ranch. When engaged in such pursuits, I didn't see rabbits or foxes but gunfighters of a most masculine appearance, which may have contributed to my actions that day at the bank.

There were few people in the Mercantile as most had chosen
to visit the courthouse, where a local man was standing trial for
murder. I gave the teller my money, then from behind heard a
rush of footsteps followed by the command, "Throw up your
hands!"

I turned to see three men with pistols, faces partly masked
by kerchiefs but all with eyes blazing. Two hurried behind the
counter where they gathered up money in canvas bags. The
third, who seemed to be in charge, kept everyone in check and
also kept his eyes on me. Despite the danger—or perhaps because of it—my prick started to fill. I don't mean to set myself
down as naïve or untried, for I wasn't. I'd certainly gotten up
to things with men on the ranch. But in this particular man, the
outlaw in charge, I saw something more: the same dark allure
I'd attributed to my imaginary gunslingers. This bandit aroused
everything in me, and I was powerless to stop it. As his cohorts
collected their loot, the man and I held a gaze. I enjoyed the fullness between my legs, and I figured him to be hard, too.

As I stood there with a stiff prick, I spotted a clerk crouched
unnoticed in a side doorway, his rifle aimed at the outlaw who
stirred me. Then came the moment when my life forever turned.
Without considering the consequences, I drew my pistol and
shot the clerk. The outlaw turned to the intruder but didn't fire
his gun as I'd already done the deed. He looked at me, taking in
the gun I held, and I saw in his eyes a great emotion. But then
his cohorts had gathered all the money and rushed to his side.
He motioned for them to leave, then hesitated and looked at me
again. I stood very still, holding my pistol, not knowing if I'd
killed a man. The outlaw nodded in such a way as to encourage
me to join him, and I did, rushing out to my horse. When the
gang rode from town, it was stronger by one.

The robbery had taken place in the late morning, and we

rode hard until the sun had crossed the sky and begun to set. I knew we had crossed the Kansas border into Missouri, but my surroundings were unfamiliar.

We rode deep into a canyon where trees grew thick along a small stream. Following the stream, we came to a clearing with a house and barn. Neither could be called fine, but after our long ride, they appeared most welcome. When the others stopped at the barn and dismounted, I did likewise.

During the ride, the outlaw I'd saved had removed his kerchief. He was a handsome devil, clean-shaven, with strong features. Larger in build than the others, he stood lean and hard, and once again I felt a stir.

"We've got us a new man," he told the others. "What's your name, boy?"

As he waited for me to speak my predicament truly settled on me. Perhaps it was his voice, perhaps it was his declaration that the gang had a new member. I don't know exactly what rendered me speechless, only that it overpowered me.

The outlaw saw my distress. "Easy now." He put an arm around my shoulder, which only made things worse. "See to the horses," he told the others, and they took the animals into the barn. My outlaw—for I now felt him to be mine—held me there a moment longer, then said we should go inside.

The house offered the comforts of home but looked as if a woman's touch had been absent for some time. It held two rooms, one with stove, table, chairs, and the like, the other most likely a bedroom.

"I'm Abel Judson," he told me. "The others are Samuel and Jacob, my brothers. Being oldest, I'm in charge. Being smartest also." He let me go, and I sank shuddering into a chair. "Reckon you never killed a man."

"No," I said. "All my gunslinging has been at rabbits and

such. Today I shot on impulse. There was no thinking on it."

"Most shooting is that way. I'd venture if a man stopped to think on it, he'd be rendered dead."

"But he was..." I stopped there, afraid to say the man had been in the right. Never mind the bags of money, I feared to challenge the right and wrong of it. And I had done wrong as well, so I spoke of that.

"This morning I was a cowhand. Now I'm a bank robber."

"Not even that. You've joined us, but the others must agree to sharing the money with you."

"I can't go home again," I said, as the notion struck me. So many things were coming to mind now. I felt cold, near sick.

"Tell me your name," Abel said. "I suspect you can recall what it is."

"Cullen Platt."

He sat next to me and shook my hand. "You're a remarkable young man, Cullen Platt. I appreciate your coming to my aid."

I had no more words. Abel stood, took a bottle from a cabinet, and poured me a drink. It was hard liquor and it seared my insides, which I welcomed. My boyhood days had truly come to an end. In the most awful way, I had become a man.

When the brothers came in, they prepared supper, but I didn't have an appetite. I was let into the bedroom, where I fell fast asleep, but I was awakened sometime later feeling someone had joined me. It was so dark that all was done by touch, but I knew it was Abel. He undid my britches, pulled down my drawers, and rubbed my bottom. "Stay quiet," was all he said as he rolled me onto my stomach. He mounted me, and I felt his hard prick poke at my backside. The thing was wet. He had prepared himself in some way so it went in easily, and he fucked me then and there.

As I had plenty of experience with men, I welcomed Abel's

attention. My cock quickly rose. He thrust quick and rough, as if greatly in need. He grunted, and I felt him squirt into me. As I received him, I let go as well, spurting a goodly amount into the bedding.

Abel took some time to finish, and I enjoyed the feel of him upon me. Once I had spent my load and begun to regain myself, I thought I might grow to like outlaw life.

When it ended, nothing was said. Like the cowboys on the ranch, he simply pulled out and left me bare. I lay recalling every moment of the fuck while I heard him snore. The next morning, when I awoke to coffee brewing and bacon on the stove, there was no indication a fucking had taken place during the night.

After breakfast, the money was counted, and everyone was pleased it came to twelve-thousand dollars in cash and gold. "What say we give young Cullen here a share as he saved my life?" Abel said.

If the brothers disagreed, they didn't show it. Both nodded. I suspect they were in awe of Abel.

"This land here is unknown," he offered, as he put my share in front of me. "We travel far to do our business, then retreat here to safety. You can never tell of this place or it'll be our end."

I took this in and readily agreed, propelled by nothing more than my personal interest in Abel Judson.

The others saw fit to discuss the robbery, which seemed a lesson toward committing the next one. Ideas were set forth as to a new bank, and Jacob, the youngest, suggested the possibility of robbing a train. At length he told how a gang had ridden as passengers, then done the robbing while onboard. Abel said it was a bad idea, as marshals were likely to be stationed on trains now, and the gang would be held captive. "Banks are what we know best," he declared, putting an end to the discussion. He announced his intention to bathe and suggested I do likewise. The brothers weren't asked, and I saw how they knew not to question or put upon their elder. So I accompanied Abel on foot up the stream a distance, far from the house, deeper into the canyon.

We stopped where an outcropping had made a pool, and Abel silently undressed. I watched him shed it all, his union suit finally, until he stood bare. He took hold of his hard prick, pulling on it some before wading into the water.

It wasn't a large stream, the water no more than thigh deep. Abel splashed a bit, then sat and called for me to join him and clean up. Of course I knew he wanted to fuck me. I'd already grown hard at the sight of his body, and when I shed my clothes and my cock popped forward, he let out a hoot. "Lookie there what you got. Come in here and give me that."

I waded in to him, the water cold. When I reached him he took me at the hips and guided me forward until my cock was at his mouth, and then he opened to me. Feeling his suck, I immediately spent into his throat. He took it all down. I couldn't help bucking into him, which he seemed to like. I was frantic with my spurts and doubly excited looking down at his mouth on my prick.

After he had taken it all, he played with my spent rod a bit then let go. "Turn around," he said, and pulled me into the water so my back was to him. He got me down on his lap so his prick could go up me. I let out a cry as I felt it in my bowels. He laughed loud. "I mean to have you often," he said as he pushed into me. "A pretty young fellow such as you is very much to my liking. You'll have many a fuck as part of the gang, and I'll always protect you."

He reached around to my chest and felt for my titties, rubbing and pinching as his thrusts continued. For some time we went on this way until he grew frantic beneath me, began to buck, then let out a roar and came. His deep call echoed in the canyon, so loudly I wondered if they heard back at the house. If so, they were sure to know we were fucking, for how could brothers not know the nature of their own? Abel's spurts were long and ample, and I grew excited by what he was doing to me. My cock rose again, as it was wont to do at the slightest encouragement, and it flapped about as he fucked me. There was plenty of splashing, but finally Abel finished, and we quieted. His head rested against my back, and I heard him breathe heavy.

He held me at the hips, his grip gentle, everything about us quiet, serene as the forest. I noted birds calling, the sun upon us. It made me quite happy. As Abel righted himself, he reached around to feel for me and found my hard cock. "You're up again," he said, and with that he worked me much as I did myself when there was nobody around to fuck. His prick had softened a bit inside me but still remained, and I squirmed on the thing while he pulled on my cock. Minutes later, I felt the wonderful rise and issued new spurts into the water. They floated to the surface, little white dots surrounding us. After Abel emptied me, he played with my prick and laughed at the gobs of spunk in the water.

When he let me go, we waded to the middle of the stream and did our washing. He was a sight to behold, thick dark fur all up his front from cock to shoulders, formidable thighs and arms. I decided then and there he was the very man I had imagined so often.

When he caught me looking more than bathing, he chuckled and came over and washed me. He seemed to appreciate having his hands on my body. He spent considerable time cleaning my cock and balls, then turned me around and bent me forward to wash my bottom. I felt his fingers on my buttocks then up and down my crack. He parted me, and I knew he was looking at my hole. His finger poked at it then pushed in, and he worked me a bit. "Fuckhole," he said. "I'm going to get into you again before we go back to the others."

I didn't think an older man would be up to having another fuck so soon after the first, but Abel wasn't an ordinary man. I couldn't tell his age but ventured him to be past thirty-five, such were his worldliness and the lines on his face. He might be twice my age, I thought as he continued to work my hole. I had turned eighteen not three months before, but I found I liked his being older. I felt a security in it, even in the midst of a gang of robbers. I knew that whatever adventures we faced, he'd look out for me.

Abel withdrew his finger, and when I turned I saw his cock was up again. "I'll fuck you on the shore," he declared, and led me to a tree where he had me bend over and grasp it. He mounted me from behind while he stood.

This time the fuck was a long one. He thrust steadily in and out of me for a good while, gripping me at the waist as he drove his cock deep inside. Sometimes he pushed all the way in and held fast, then grinded against me for a bit, and this I truly enjoyed, his big thing working around inside my passage. Then he'd resume his stroke. On occasion his prick popped out, and he rode it up my crack, rubbing on me before driving it back inside my hole. All these things worked him up, and I could tell he was trying to draw more up out of his balls.

My hole was raw when he finally spurted inside me. My legs ached, my bottom was sore, but Abel seemed unfazed by his effort. Then his spunk arrived, and he let out a yell unlike his earlier roar: a cry of great relief, as if he were pleased not only with the feel of the cum but that it had at last arrived. He pushed into me hard as he spurted and kept at it even when his stuff stopped coming. I think he didn't want the fuck to end, but it did at last and he withdrew. I turned to see him covered in sweat, his fur glistening in the sun, his great cock hanging between his legs. Without a word, he ran to the stream and jumped in.

When we returned to the house, his brothers offered no comment. Abel suggested they go to the stream to bathe, which they did. I suspected he wanted me alone with him.

We settled at the table, and he set to cleaning his gun. I thought of my own weapon but didn't take it up as it brought to mind the bad turn my life had taken. Instead I watched Abel. After he'd finished, he took out a map, which he studied for some time.

"There are banks in Ellsworth and Hays City we haven't robbed," he told me. "In a few days we'll set out for one. You can ride along and take part."

Until then I hadn't considered the next robbery, and I reminded myself that I wasn't an outlaw. I didn't want anyone's money, for I knew firsthand of the hard work required for a day's pay. I considered telling Abel this, but he went on about his plan, and I knew he had no idea toward anything but his own way. I told myself I had no choice, that my shooting the clerk meant there would be no other life for me. I was fortunate to be taken up as I had. So when we rode into Kansas to rob the bank at Ellsworth, I went along.

Abel made use of me each day with a good hard fuck and sometimes did it twice. He also sucked my prick a good deal. It became his practice to get at me in bed each night, but sometimes he did it early in the morning as well, awakening with his cock hard and making use of it. Other times he caught me bathing or in the barn or simply got out his cock for a quick one when he happened upon me most anywhere. The brothers often saw us, and when they did they went their own way although young Jacob lingered a bit one time, rubbing his crotch as he looked on.

So I was much fucked and happy, but then came the trip to Ellsworth. I would've rather stayed behind but knew not to ask, as such a thing was a woman's way. Abel charged me with watching over the horses while the others committed the robbery. I took this to be his understanding that I was no real outlaw. I was pleased to ride with him, but my innards cramped up as I thought about the robbery.

The three brothers entered the bank, and I heard Abel shout, "Throw up your hands," then nothing more until Samuel and Jacob rushed out with sacks of loot. They mounted their horses, and we waited. Then came a gunshot, and my heart sank. A moment of agony passed until Abel dashed out and leapt onto his horse. And then we were off.

As before, we rode steadily to Missouri. We made camp at dusk and later that night Abel took me some distance from the fire, put down a blanket, and had him a good fuck.

It wasn't until his cock went up me that I felt at peace. The robbery had brought up a strong fear in me; I detested the danger Abel craved, hated the idea he might be lost to me. I felt alone and scared until he put his prick inside me. He was rough and quick, and I knew it had to do with his outlaw ways, but I only cared that he was fucking me. I spurted while he ground into me. When he spent his own load, it was with loud grunts, and I felt his seed warm in me.

After Abel pulled out and rolled me over, he took my cock in his mouth and sucked until I hardened again and burst forth with new spurts, which he gulped down. After he sucked me dry we lay alongside each other. In my comfort I grew bold enough to tell him my confession. "I'm no bank robber," I said. "Even as I hold the horses I worry after you. I've become very attached and would hate to lose you."

"Would you go free instead?" he asked.

"I don't want to leave you. Besides, I'm now a wanted man."

"You could be free of it, go west, change your name."

"Don't you want me?"

Abel went silent, and I thought I'd gone too far. Listening to his breathing, I hoped he understood. He said no more but put a hand to my thigh, which told me all.

In the morning he didn't fuck me. We rose with the sun and rode home, reaching the house at midday. He didn't say a word until he declared we would bathe. He took a blanket, and we went upstream.

Abel stripped naked and went into the water, ignoring me, it seemed. Uncertain, I stripped and waded in, cock limp. He washed himself and so did I. He pulled on his cock as if to encourage the thing. I approached him, turned, bent, and parted my buttocks to invite him in. He obliged, and as his prick had grown hard, he put it inside me.

Standing in the water, we fucked for all to see, and once again I knew happiness. I thought he did too, that he might like his robbing but he liked his fucking more. As he thrust in and out, he reached around and took hold of my now-hard cock, pulling at it while he fucked. As I unloaded my spunk, I cried out and his thrusts grew urgent. Then he issued great long spurts into my passage.

Afterward, we lay in the water and he played his hands over the whole of me. I saw in his eyes that he loved me, but I knew a man couldn't say such a thing to another man. So I took comfort in his touch. He rubbed me gently, poked and prodded some. He massaged my titties until they grew hard, then got a hand under me and put a finger up my hole. He seemed content to have it in me, to take his time. I knew he wanted to fuck again.

The sun was nearly down when he grew ready. He had me on a blanket on the shore and put two fingers inside me. His cock stood erect, but he still played with me, taking my balls in one hand while he prodded my hole. "I would have you with me always," he said, and my heart leapt, for this was a true declaration.

"I would be with you always," I replied.

With that he rolled me onto my stomach and gave me a long fuck.

The day of reckoning came in Newton, Kansas, some months later when shots were fired inside a bank during a robbery. I held the horses and waited, fear choking me. Barely able to breathe, I saw Abel tumble from the door, but the others didn't follow. He had no loot in hand. "Ride," he told me, as he climbed into his saddle. When I looked at the bank, he said, "Samuel and Jacob are dead," and rode away. I could only follow.

During the night, we reached Missouri but didn't stop. At dawn, when we arrived at the house, Abel appeared grief-stricken. We dismounted, but he didn't go into the house. Instead he stormed about, beset with a pain so great, an anger so immense I didn't dare come near him. He drew his pistol and fired it until it was empty, then tossed it away. After this he quieted, slumped to the ground, and I went to him.

He crouched in the dirt, and when I put a hand to his shoulder, he grabbed me and pushed me onto my back. He climbed atop me and humped as if having a fuck. He swore and said all manner of foul things, which I knew not to take to heart. I started to undress him, and when he saw me agreeable to his need he stood and stripped naked then and there. I did likewise, saw his hard cock, and knew his pain had settled where he might make use of it. So I got on all fours, and he mounted me from behind in the dirt.

It was a rough fuck but a good one, his only solace for his great loss, and when his cum released inside me he roared like a wounded animal. After he finished, he pulled out and staggered to his feet, going about the place naked like a madman. I managed to corral him and get him into the house, where I put him to bed. I brought him whiskey, which he drank until sleep came.

Abel slept the entire day then awakened at night. He came out of the bedroom stark naked, dirty, and coarse, still in the grip of pain. "Drop your britches. I'm in need of a fuck."

I bared my bottom, and he took me standing as I leaned over a chair. His thrust was steady, and I knew he'd need plenty of fucking in the days ahead as it was his sole comfort. It took him time to spend, surely the result of the liquor and fatigue, but at last he grunted and emptied into me. Then he left me to go upstream to wash.

Two days passed before Abel would talk to me about the failed robbery and loss of his kin. We ate and slept and fucked. Nothing more. But as a third day dawned and he started to put his cock inside me while we were in bed, I turned to face him. "You told me once I could change my name, go west, and become free. You could do the same. We could buy a ranch with our robbery money. I know that life and you can surely learn. We can have a new beginning, but I fear if we stay here it'll drive you mad. Take the memory of your brothers and go with me to California."

"Roll over."

"There's a time to fuck and a time to talk. You've had fucking for two days. Now you must talk."

Abel shut his eyes, and I knew he resisted all because he wasn't a man of words. He reached for me again, and at first I pulled back, then saw it wasn't sexual. He put his arm around me and held me close, and as I felt a shudder pass through him, I had my answer.

1 A.M. COWBOY

Simon Sheppard

So you who hate the USA,
You commies, atheists, and gays,
You'd better run, startin' today,
'Cause me and God are on our way.

There was a tremendous roar from the audience, stamping
and whistling and clapping, a tumult that quickly morphed
into an earsplitting chant of "U-S-A...U-S-A."

Who'd have imagined, thought the Stetsoned man in the
spotlight, *that L.A. was so full of Christian conservatives? So
full of MY people?*

Across town, and an hour or two later, Harry Deering hopped
out of a taxi and, ignoring what he at least imagined was the
supercilious sneer of the uniformed doorman, pulled a slip of
paper from his pocket and checked the room number.

The heels of his cowboy boots clicked on the highly polished floor as he headed across the lobby toward the bank of elevators. He was familiar with the place. He'd been there, more than once, to service a Scientologist superstar who was cheating on his new wife. He knew that, as little as he felt he belonged there, if he kept going, looked like he knew what he was doing, nobody, no one at all, would stop him to ask, "Hey, aren't you a goddamn hustler?"

He picked up the phone beside the elevators and punched in the room number.

"Hello?"

"Hey. It's Brett," said Harry. "I'm on my way up."

"Brett? Oh, yeah. Okay. C'mon up."

The coast was clear. Harry felt excited as the elevator headed to the penthouse floor. It was stupid, he knew that, but just being in the presence of conspicuous wealth still had an effect on him. Didn't matter how many times now he'd fucked millionaires' asses—money gave him a hard-on. Which made him perfect for his job.

There was a knock. Craig McCormack looked through the peephole, then opened the door. Well, the kid was a little overdone, no doubt about it. He'd ordered up a cowboy from the agency, but this boy was sheer Joe Buck: hip-slung jeans, embroidered boots, white cowboy hat, and—God help us—a fringed buckskin jacket. But serviceable. Nicely handsome face, a little on the rugged side, but something boyish about it, too. The kid was, in fact, fuckable. Nice and fuckable.

"C'mon in."

Harry felt a little thrill of recognition. Wasn't that...? Yeah, it was. He was damn near sure, though the singer was shorter than he looked on TV. His last single, "Me and God," had rocketed to the top of the country charts. Craig McCormack. That guy was worth money, plenty of it. *And* he was married, to that soap actress, what's-her-name. Not that Harry would ever blackmail someone—the thought never even crossed his mind—but if he was discreet and played his cards right, this could become a regular gig, like spanking the Scientologist. Big tips. Big money. His uncut dick snaked down his denim-clad leg.

"C'mon in," the man said. "I'm Sam." Harry wondered whether McCormack figured he hadn't been recognized, whether he just hoped so, or whether he knew Harry had clocked him but expected him to play along. Maybe any of that. Harry was good at hiding his emotions, and that talent had served him well.

"Thanks." He consciously drawled it.

"What was your name again?"

"Brett."

"Drink?"

"Whatcha got…Sam?"

"Whiskey? That's what I'm drinking."

"Sure, rocks."

McCormack kept an eye on the boy as he poured him a drink. Brett, or whatever his name was, took off his cowboy hat and threw it on a chair. "Mind if I sit?" the hustler asked.

"Make yourself comfortable."

The boy sprawled in the other chair, legs spread wide, head thrown back, stroking his shoulder-length brown hair. It was supposed to look seductive. It did.

The guy offered him a drink. There was an unopened bottle of Cristal in a cooler by the bed. Harry liked expensive champagne, one of a number of tastes he'd picked up since hitting L.A. But

all the client offered him was a whiskey—though Harry as-
sumed, correctly, that it would be a very good whiskey—and he
figured it would be both polite and good for his image not to ask
about the Cristal.

He sat in the chair and spread his legs, letting one hand
trail down to his crotch, fingers just brushing his basket. Now
the singer would have to serve *him*, and he figured—also correctly—that wouldn't bother his client a bit. Since he'd left Elko,
he'd learned quite a bit about human nature.

So he was expected to serve some hustler a drink? Didn't this
kid know who he *was*? No, of course he didn't. The buckskin-
jacketed boy just sat there caressing his crotch. And now, as he
walked over to this Brett, drinks in hand, Craig McCormack felt
his own dick swell up.

"Here y'go." The boy looked out from half-closed eyes and
grabbed the whiskey. Craig had to admit, this boy knew what
he was doing. Of course, the boy had no way of knowing about
the other Brett, *his* Brett.

He'd had an enormous crush on Brett Moore through high
school, had even joined the Young Republicans just to be close
to him. He'd never gotten in Brett's pants, though, and the last
time they'd met, years later, it hadn't gone well. Craig had been
back in Chapel Hill to celebrate his father's being made a full
professor at the university. His soon-to-go-platinum album, *No
Goddamn Liberal*, had recently come out, and Brett—who had
become a card-carrying member of the ACLU—had thrown the
lyrics of the title song right back at him.

"*But no goddamn liberal can tell me to smile / at two freaky
fruits as they walk down the aisle*? Craig, what the hell is that
about?"

Craig had laid his hand on Brett's shoulder. He still wanted

him so much, and now that he was a big star... "Brett," he'd
said, "it's just show business, right?"

Brett had brushed his hand away. "Fuck you, Craig."

"Brett..."

"No, I mean it. Fuck you."

Actually, Brett had misquoted the song. It was *force me to
smile.*

McCormack had gotten a faraway look in his eyes. It was time
to bring him back to the business at hand.

"Thanks for the drink, man," Harry said. He gave his crotch
a squeeze. "Anything I can do for *you?*" Craig was standing
right between his outstretched legs. Harry's eyes trailed down-
ward. The singer still wasn't hard, at least not visibly. Time to
up the ante. He unzipped his fly.

"You're really a cowboy?" McCormack asked.

"Yeah, rode horses and all that stuff. Back in Nevada." This
wasn't going the way Harry had planned. Still, it was the guy's
dime, and he was a superstar. And there'd been other times
when he'd gone to some john's house and all the man wanted to
do was talk. Harry took this not as a criticism of his attractive-
ness, but as a sign of how fucked up some guys were.

But Craig McCormack? Hell, Harry wanted a big star like him
to suck his cock. "Yeah," he repeated, "horses and all that stuff."

The night was beginning to catch up with him. The concert had
been exhausting—most of them were, these days—and it was his
fourth whiskey. No, fifth. Time to get what he was paying for.
He put down the drink and unbuttoned his fly.

"Okay, cowboy. Blow me." He reached into his boxers
and pulled out his still-soft dick. But the hustler didn't make a
move, just sat there with his eyes still half-closed.

"No," Brett said, between sips of Wild Turkey. "*You* blow *me*."

Harry knew from experience that these married guys claimed to just want to be sucked off, but what they really wanted was a mouthful of dick. Preferably a big hard dick like his. He fished it out of his pants. It was stiff and thick, the foreskin still half-covering the shiny head, and while he wasn't much of a connoisseur, he knew most of his clients found it gorgeous.

And he was right again. McCormack's dick had started to get hard, and after a few seconds of hesitation, he dropped to his knees and, drink still in his hand, began to nuzzle Harry's cock. But instead of putting his wet lips on the shaft, all McCormack seemed to want to do was lie with his head in the hustler's lap and murmur, "Brett...Brett."

"G'wan, mister. Suck it. You know you want to."

McCormack snapped out of his trance and slid his lips over the partly obscured head of Harry's dick.

That was more like it.

He had to admit it: Sucking the cowboy's cock was nice. A nice, hard, hot piece of meat in his mouth. He reached up and unbuckled the boy's broad belt, then tugged open the waistband of his jeans. The kid wasn't wearing underwear. And he hadn't trimmed his bush, either. Craig liked that. He hated when guys trimmed down their crotches, or worse, shaved. What the hell was that about? It wasn't like they had cunt lips to expose.

He tugged at Brett's jeans, and the hustler raised his hips so Craig could slide them down to mid-thigh. Nice, hairy legs, too. Trim, muscled. He actually could picture this guy on a horse.

Never taking his mouth off Brett's cock, he slid his hands down over the hustler's knees, down his shins, till he reached the boy's boots. He ran his palms over the heels, the embroidered leather, the pointy toes. Cowboy. The hustler's cock throbbed against his tongue.

Not a bad cocksucker at all. Singing wasn't the only use Mc-Cormack had found for his mouth. Should he say something? Something encouraging? Something demeaning? Drawl out, "Yeah, that's it. Suck that cock," stuff like that?

Harry did, after all, believe in giving his customers good value. It was the way to build a steady clientele. If that paunchy software billionaire got off on being dressed up in diapers (and he did), then Pampers it was.

And yeah, the fringed jacket might have been a bit much, trotted out on request. But he hadn't lied. He'd been on plenty of horses back in Elko, back when he'd been a teenage farmhand shoveling shit. He'd had a pickup with a gun rack, too, until he wrapped it around a tree while he was wired on crystal.

Not exactly Clint Eastwood, maybe, but then, Harry kinda doubted Eastwood would fuck Craig McCormack's face.

Though in Hollywood, you never knew for sure....

The guy had a nice, stiff cowboy dick. A real mouthful. But Mc-Cormack was woozy from drink, tired from a long night. He'd had it with kneeling down. He took his mouth off the big cock and struggled to his feet. Standing over the hustler, he unzipped his pants and pulled down his boxers. His hard-on sprang free, and he grabbed at it and started squeezing.

The cowpoke-hustler looked up at him with narrowed eyes. "Hey, Sam," he said, "I don't suck dick."

"But I'm paying."

"It wasn't what we agreed to." The kid seemed like he was

trying for "laconic," like Clint Fucking Eastwood. "And besides, real men don't suck dick."

"Get on the bed, then. On all fours." Like a horsie.

Brett grew somewhat less laconic. "And I don't get fucked, either."

"I ain't gonna fuck you."

"I don't get fucked," Harry repeated, just to make things clear. Though he had gotten fucked. Plenty of times. When he'd been cold and hungry enough. In the men's room at the Greyhound station in Elko. And by that rancher's son he'd thought he'd been in love with. Way back when.

But McCormack had said he wasn't going to fuck him, and Harry didn't want this session to go badly. Big stars—especially big stars in the closet—meant big money. So he pulled off his boots and tugged off his tight jeans.

"Leave your jacket on." McCormack's million-dollar voice was sounding slurry.

Harry Deering got onto the bed, on all fours.

The boy had a real nice ass, no doubt about that. Craig got behind him, behind that terrific butt.

"Okay, cowboy…," he said, but left the sentence unfinished. He leaned down, stuck out his tongue, and licked Brett's tailbone. He reached around the boy, the fringe hanging from the jacket brushing the back of his hand. He found a nipple and stroked it through the boy's T-shirt. Brett made appreciative noises, and Craig ran his mouth down the hustler's hairy buttcrack till he felt warm softness against his tongue.

"Oh, yeah," Brett moaned, though how sincerely was hard to say. Craig flicked his tongue against the boy's hole, then began licking up and down.

This was it. This was what he really wanted. He thought of all the millions of people in all the audiences he'd sung to. They didn't know—how could they? But this is what he longed for. Dirty fucking hot hole. Man hole. He took his fingers from Brett's tit, backed off a little, and grabbed both asscheeks, spreading them wide. The kid's ass opened up nicely, showing a glistening darker pink in its depths. He stuck his tongue as far in as he could.

So that was it. The great, patriotic, butch dude liked to eat ass. And liked it, apparently, a lot. Well, Harry had seen a lot worse. He'd dressed men up in women's lingerie before he fucked them. He'd pissed on his clients, even crapped on one or two. Whatever. Whatever the job required. Within reason. And depending on the fee. But this? Fuck, getting rimmed felt so good, he'd do it for free.

Only he wasn't doing it for free. Not by a long shot.

"Oh, man, that feels great," he moaned, partly because that's what the occasion demanded, partly because it did feel great. He lowered his head to the mattress and reached back to stroke his still-stiff dick. Might as well relax and enjoy this. Though he hoped the guy would be satisfied soon. He had an early class at USC the next morning, a philosophy class, a pisser.

When Craig McCormack really got into eating ass, the rest of the world—the troubling, confusing world—ceased to exist. There was only that warm, wet contact. That was all that mattered. He pushed his tongue as far inside the boy's guts as he could, then pulled out, running his lips down the seam of the hustler's furry perineum, licking the big dangling balls, then back up again, to the hole. Brett was jacking himself off now, which meant he was enjoying it, too, and even though Craig was paying, he was glad.

He almost didn't hear it, and he almost wished he hadn't. "That's it," the hustler said. "Eat my ass, Craig."

The kid knew who he really was, then.

He pulled his mouth away.

He wished he hadn't said it, of course. He didn't know why he had. How he'd let it slip. Still, McCormack freaking out like that was sort of silly. Did he really think someone as famous as he was could go around hiring hustlers and not be recognized? Stupider still, he was into country boys, exactly the sort most likely to know who he was.

Harry acted as though he hadn't let the singer's name slip, as though he had no idea why the probing mouth had left his ass. "Go on, Sam," he said. "Lick it."

But McCormack had gotten to his feet. "Get up, Brett," he said.

The singer's face was angry, yes, but he also seemed a little scared. Maybe it was all that booze.

"Hey," said Harry, "sorry, man."

"This isn't some kind of fucking shakedown, is it?"

Harry was a little hurt. He'd never considered such a thing. He was, after all, a whore, not a blackmailer. And besides, that kind of reputation would be bad for business.

"Jesus, man, no." Harry was crouching on the bed, his dick deflated.

"Because if it is…" Craig McCormack reached into a dresser drawer. Fuck, did he have a gun? Well, of course he did—Harry remembered that song of his, what was it? "Freedom Is a .44." *And if you take my piece from me, you'll have to pry it from my cold, dead hands.* Harry also remembered, oddly, his mother, dying from cancer, listening over and over to Craig McCormack's Christmas album.

But McCormack didn't pull a gun from the drawer. He stood with a pile of bills in his hand. "Here," he said, "take it. Get out. And forget this ever happened."

McCormack's cockhead had retreated into its long foreskin. He had a pretty nice-looking dick. Not as big as Harry's—kind of small, actually—but suckable.

"How about I go down on you?" Harry asked. "To show no hard feelings?"

"Go on. Take this and get the hell out."

McCormack watched as the hustler stripped in reverse. Too bad things had to end this way. He was a good-looking kid. And a real cowboy, too, or at least so he said. Oh, well, these things happened sometimes. He poured himself another drink, not offering Brett one.

When the hustler was fully dressed, he stood there for a minute like he was expecting something, like maybe free tickets to his next show.

"Go on," Craig said between sips, "get out. And don't forget your hat."

Jesus, what *was* that? For a weird minute, Harry thought Craig McCormack was going to cry. But no, it was just that his face was all flushed with liquor. Probably.

Oh, well, he'd gotten paid, no problem. More than he'd expected, actually, though whether that was intentional, he had no idea.

And now he could take a cab home, take this shit off, get some rest.

The hotel lobby was near empty when he left, and nobody gave him a second glance.

Outside the hotel window, most of L.A. was asleep. McCormack watched the cowboy go, switched on the radio, then turned it off again. He stripped down, turned off the lights, and crawled into bed.

He inhaled deeply. He could still smell the scent of the boy's asshole. He reached down and stroked his hardening cock. It was a comforting feeling, the touch of his own hand sliding the foreskin back and forth, back and forth. He thought of the way Brett's asshole looked, the way it had tasted when it yielded to his tongue. Back and forth, back and forth. He said it aloud: "I want to eat ass." His cock was hard as a rock now, close to coming. His tongue against the boy's soft insides. Horsie. The spotlight. Him walking home from high school with Brett, almost getting up the courage to tell him how he felt—but then the moment had passed. The roar of his fans. Brett's dick. Hard cock, hairy ass, pink hole. He came then, not so much squirting as oozing cum, a big sopping handful. Ordinarily he wiped off with a Kleenex. But he just brought his wet hand to his mouth, his cum's saltiness joining the lingering scent of Brett's ass, and licked his palm clean. Brett. He was drunk, exhausted, nearly asleep. Brett.

Sometimes he wished...

Sometimes he wished...

WESTON'S SPREAD

Jude Gray

Alex Weston's hazel eyes swept across the wide-open land stretching outside his kitchen window, and he shivered in the cold October morning. He had just added wood to the kitchen stove, so it would be some time before the room warmed up. As he turned from the window, he put on a pot of coffee and crossed bare arms over his hairy chest. He moved around the cold kitchen, getting breakfast organized and slapping his arms as he struggled to wake up. Being cold and naked was the best way he knew to fully awaken himself each day. Most mornings he woke up in his huge, warm bed with a painful hard-on begging to be drained of piss and his hot, sticky seed. To keep himself from lingering in bed, he had taken to masturbating in the outhouse after relieving his bulging bladder. By sitting in the stink and cold of the outhouse to release his pent-up hormones rather than the comfort of his bed he wasn't tempted to tarry too long and waste the daylight.

On this morning, with the lightest touch of frost on the ground, Alex stood with his butt dangerously close to the stove as he warmed his bare backside. He blew a stray lock of wavy dark hair off his forehead and decided it was time to get moving.

Just more than a year ago Alex's grandfather had passed on and willed the entire ranch, what everyone in these parts knew as Weston's Spread, to his unwed, twenty-four-year-old grandson, his only surviving family. Alex's grandfather had raised him, as he'd lost his parents and two younger siblings to disease years ago. When his grandfather had released his final breath, Alex felt something break within him. He was alone for good now, no one to turn to for help with the ranch or to talk with when the sun fell behind the foothills and the long, dark night took the open land.

Shaking his head to clear away his negative thoughts, Alex took a deep breath and burst out of the warming kitchen into the brisk air.

"Yikes!" he cried, his balls pulling up and his hard-on quickly retreating at the rude slap of cold air. He dashed to the outhouse and jumped inside, slamming the door behind him. He stood before the smooth, wooden seat and released a long, steady stream of piss into the dank, wet depths.

When Alex had finished, he turned to sit on the seat and took himself in his hand, stroking his member back to life. His cock unfurled slowly, reluctant to expose itself to the cold. He closed his eyes and stroked harder, willing himself back to life. His thoughts fastened on images of faceless, nameless men: burly, hairy men. Their cocks and balls swung low between their legs, and in his mind he found dozens of ways to please them. He was a great lover of men, but only in his mind, for Alex had never been with one. He'd had a woman once—a whore in town—and while the experience was somewhat pleasurable, he wasn't eager to engage in it again. He'd always been drawn to the rugged ranch hands his grandfather had employed before money became a problem and the older Weston had to let them go one by one.

Alex wrapped his other rough, callused hand around his hairy balls and pulled them taut, stretching the sac into the dark pit of the outhouse. He tipped his head against the rear wall and sighed, his strokes growing quicker and his grip tightening. His breathing picked up until his exhalations matched the rhythm of his fist and his breath plumed from his lips in the cold air.

Just before he could finish himself off, the door jerked open, flooding the tiny room with light and cold air. Alex gasped and hunched forward, trying in vain to cover his pulsing erection as he blinked in the glare of the morning sun.

"Hey!" he snapped. "What the hell do you think you're doing?"

"Oh! Sorry!" a deep, male voice replied. "Didn't know anyone was in here."

Alex squinted at the dark outline before him. He couldn't see the man's features as the sun shone behind him, but he could make out a silhouette of broad shoulders and a trim waist. A cowboy hat sat on the man's head, and Alex heard the scuffle of boots on gravel as the stranger shifted his weight.

"Do you mind?" Alex said, his erection quickly deflating. "It's cold."

"Yep, yep." The stranger eased the door shut, saying again, "Sorry."

Alex paused for a moment, his eyes closed and his mind racing. He had no clothes with him and didn't know if the man was alone.

"Hey, you out there," Alex called.

"Yep." The stranger's voice came back from right outside the door, and Alex jumped. The least he could have done was step a few feet away!

"Are you alone?"

"Just me and my horse," the man said.

"Okay." Alex took a breath and pushed the door open. He stepped outside and shivered in the wind, cupping his hands over his crotch. Moving quickly, he ran into the house and slammed the door behind him.

After quickly dressing, Alex threw on his tan leather coat lined with sheep wool and dropped his brown Stetson on his head. He stepped outside in time to see the stranger emerge from the outhouse buttoning up his worn denim pants. Anger sizzled in Alex's chest as he walked quickly across the yard. Just as he reached the man, however, he noticed the stranger's square jaw and clear blue eyes, and his determined step faltered.

"You could have knocked," Alex said, his voice sounding less angry than he would have liked. He felt small and childish standing before this tall, broad-shouldered man with the tanned, handsome face.

The stranger smiled, showing white teeth through a dark blond beard. His blue eyes crinkled at the corners as he lifted a hand and slid his hat back from his forehead. His torso appeared thick and strong beneath a black leather jacket also lined with sheepskin. Large, tan leather gloves covered his hands. His denim pants were faded across the crotch and ass, hugging every curve of his package.

"I'm real sorry about storming in on you like that," the man said with genuine feeling. "I had to go real bad, and it looked like nobody was around." He ducked his head and watched Alex from the corner of his eye, grinning slightly. "I surprised you pretty good, huh?"

"Well, yeah," Alex stammered. He blushed as his anger

drained away and embarrassment rushed to fill the void. "I don't get a lot of visitors."

"I guess not, bein' set back from the road so far," the man said. He removed a glove and stuck out his hand. "Tucker Matthews."

Alex watched his own hand get swallowed up by Tucker's huge, hair-covered paw. "Alex Weston."

"Nice to meet you, Mr. Weston," Tucker said as he pumped Alex's arm.

"Please, just call me Alex." He tried not to stare at Tucker as he withdrew his hand. His fingers radiated with heat after being engulfed by the man's tight grip. "So, you from town or something?"

"Nope, just looking for work." Tucker turned his gaze to the property surrounding them. "Nice piece of land you got here."

"Thanks." Alex looked around as well, thinking of all the work he needed to do that day. "I inherited it a year ago from my grandfather."

"Really? Just you or is there a Mrs. Weston?"

"Just me." Alex looked at his boots, suddenly shy.

"Lot of land for one man to run," Tucker stated. "Need some help?"

Alex raised his eyes. "I don't have any money, Mr. Matthews, so I can't pay you."

"I didn't ask for money. And the name's Tucker." He looked up at the house. "Just the one bedroom?"

"Huh? Oh, yeah." Alex took a breath. "If you're not asking for money, what would you be asking for?"

"Room and board. I've got nowhere to go and all the time in the world to get there. Just need a roof over my head."

Alex considered the offer for a few seconds before saying, "Deal. But I've only got the one bed."

"I don't mind sharing if you don't." His eyes seemed to pin Alex to the spot, as if daring him to mention a different arrangement.

Alex swallowed the sudden lump in his throat and shrugged, trying to act as easygoing as his new ranch hand about sharing a bed, while on the inside his stomach clenched itself into knots. "I don't mind at all. Take your horse to the stable and meet me in the kitchen for breakfast." As he watched the rugged man saunter away, he forced himself to put all concerns of sharing a bed out of his mind. He could worry about that later; the two had work to do.

After breakfast, Alex and Tucker decided to split up and work on separate chores. During the day, Alex occasionally caught himself scanning the property for his new ranch hand. He caught sight of Tucker at different places on the ranch, wiping sweat from his brow or bent over repairing a broken fence post, his hands strong and confident, his attention focused. The hours flew by, and when dusk settled on the fields, Alex headed to the house, tired but satisfied with his work. Tucker entered the warm kitchen a short while later, pulling off his boots and setting them by the fire in the living room.

As the two men prepared dinner they discussed their accomplishments. Alex was impressed with the amount of work Tucker had completed and tried not to stare too long into the man's bright blue eyes as they talked over supper. He learned a lot about Tucker's past, how he had left home at sixteen, against his father's wishes, to live off the land. He felt his cock stir each time Tucker smiled.

"I'll wash up the dishes," Tucker said after they had finished eating. "You sit back and relax."

Alex leaned back in his chair and watched Tucker's denim-hugged ass flex as he scrubbed the dishes. Tucker wore an old long-sleeve undershirt, the neck split, allowing a mass of dark blond curls to spring free. All through dinner, Alex's cock had been half erect, and now it hardened even more as he watched Tucker move through the kitchen. He regretted now not being able to finish himself off that morning in the outhouse: his balls were aching to release their load.

After Tucker finished the dishes they sat by the stove, talking about life on the road and around the ranch. Before long, both men were yawning and stretching, tired from their labor and the warm fire.

"So, where's this bed I heard tell about this morning?" Tucker finally asked, and Alex's heart pounded in his chest. He hadn't thought about the sleeping arrangements since that morning! How could he sleep next to this man with his throbbing erection?

"Uh, it's upstairs," Alex stammered nervously. "I'll make sure the fire's okay in the kitchen here. You go ahead and get ready for bed."

"Nah, I gotta use the outhouse first." Tucker reached down and squeezed his bulging crotch. "Gotta drain it before crawling into bed, you know?" He winked and walked into the cold without pulling on his coat or boots.

Alex stood in the kitchen, his mind whirling with all the possibilities that went with the phrase "drain it." Was Tucker going to masturbate out there as Alex had been trying to do when he had been interrupted that morning? He made himself busy, trying not to think about what Tucker was doing in the outhouse, where he was touching himself, or how big his cock got when he was aroused.

He pulled the top half of his all-in-ones off his arms and poured some water he had been heating on the stove into a large washbasin. Trying to keep his mind away from thoughts of Tucker's body, he began to wash himself, using a washcloth and cake of soap to clean his face, neck, torso, and armpits. The house didn't have a bathtub, so he was forced to wash up in the kitchen each night.

Blowing into his hands to warm up, Tucker stepped back inside. He took a seat at the kitchen table and silently watched Alex as he washed himself. With a nervous glance over his shoulder, Alex said, "I'd like to clean my private areas, if you don't mind."

Tucker shrugged, his eyes locked on Alex's. "I don't mind at all. Seen a lot of men's danglers in my day. Go ahead and wash away."

Hesitating briefly, Alex saw no way out of the situation without looking foolish and decided to suck up his embarrassment. Apparently men washed before each other all the time on the road. He dropped his pants then shucked his all-in-ones to the floor as well. Turning his back to Tucker, he cleared his mind and quickly washed his half-erect cock and balls then reached around to scrub the crack of his ass. He felt Tucker's eyes on his body and didn't know what to think of the attention. It was what he had longed for all his life and yet he was afraid to take the chance. He hunched over and rinsed himself off as well as he could without exposing his erection then dried off and pulled his all-in-ones back up over his body.

"You know," Tucker said with a sigh, "I think I'll clean up too. I've worked up a mighty sweat today."

"Okay," Alex replied, and started to leave the room, heading for the stairs and the relative safety of the empty bed. He could relieve his aching boner and possibly be asleep before Tucker made it to bed. "I'll give you some privacy."

"Hell, I don't need privacy," Tucker said with a grin. "Stay and talk while I clean up and we'll head upstairs together."

"Oh, uh, all right," Alex stammered. He turned awkwardly, still trying to hide the tent pole inside his baggy long johns, and sat in the chair Tucker had vacated. The seat was still warm from Tucker's firm ass, and he swiveled to hide his rising boner beneath the table as they discussed the chores Alex wanted to accomplish the following day.

He tried not to stare as Tucker stood facing him, casually removing his clothes, but his eyes dropped of their own accord when the man finally stood before him completely nude. Good Lord, he had even removed his socks! Tucker's body was fantastic. His chest was full and muscular, covered with the dark blond hair that had been poking up from beneath his undershirt. The hair traveled over his flat stomach and gathered in a darker, wild bush at his groin. His cock hung down his left thigh. A husk of foreskin hid the tip from view, but the pronounced ridge of the head was visible through the tough sheath. Alex couldn't help staring: he had never seen an uncut cock before.

Tucker slowly washed his face and armpits, his body angled so that Alex saw his long, twitching cock at all times. Raising one muscular arm and then the other and exposing the pale, hairy pits beneath, Tucker washed his entire torso, keeping up a litany of idle chitchat in the process.

After rinsing out the washrag and soaping it up again, Tucker moved his hand down to clean his crotch. He scrubbed at the hair surrounding his cock and lifted his large hairy balls to wash the area beneath, his actions riveting Alex. The man's balls looked as big as the bull's up in the pasture.

Tucker turned his upper body away and rinsed out the washrag, leaving his hips positioned to expose his soapy cock and balls. While the man was focused on the washbasin, Alex ran his eyes over his strong back muscles and the firm, round silhouette of his hairy ass. God, how he longed to touch him, run his hands

over his solid muscles. Alex's cock was so hard it ached and a
spot of precum spread along the crotch of his all-in-ones.

He shifted his weight in the chair, then dropped his jaw
as Tucker turned his back fully and lifted his left foot off the
floor to prop it on the counter near the washbasin. Reaching
back, he used a hand to pull back one firm globe of his ass and
expose his hairy, dark hole. Alex found himself four feet away
from this handsome stranger's sweaty, puckered shithole. He
had never seen a man's anus before. He stared at the wrinkled
hole and nearly gasped when the muscle opened and closed as
if Tucker were taking a deep breath through his ass. Alex's cock
banged on the underside of the table, filled to bursting with
blood, and he hissed in pain. Quickly covering up the sound
with a cough, he watched Tucker run the washrag along the
crack of his ass, lathering himself up. He couldn't take his eyes
from the man before him, no matter how hard he tried. The
muscles in Tucker's supporting right leg bunched tightly, defin-
ing themselves all the way to his foot.

A stream of soapsuds slid around the curve of Tucker's
ass and down the back of his thigh. Several tiny bubbles were
trapped in the thick hair along his leg, and Alex had to work to
swallow past a lump in his throat. If he wasn't careful he'd blow
his load just sitting there. As he raised his eyes back to Tucker's
ass, the man reached between his legs and slipped a thick, blunt
index finger inside himself. Alex's eyes widened as Tucker's finger slid in and out several times, soaping his shithole through
and through.

Tucker slowly removed his finger and, with his leg still
propped on the counter, wrung out the washrag in the basin. He
reached back and washed away the soap, wetting his finger in the
basin and slipping it inside himself again to rinse out his hole.

Alex finally tore his eyes from the man's body and stared

breathlessly at the tabletop. He watched out of the corner of his eye as Tucker lowered his leg and turned to face him. He could just make out the swinging motion of the rugged man's thick cock as he dried himself off.

"Ready for bed?" Tucker asked casually.

Alex nodded and forced himself to look up at Tucker's face, averting his eyes from the hairy body before him. Tucker's eyes were bright and his lips curled into a sexy, secret grin as he said, "Let's head upstairs then."

Tucker bent down to pick up his clothes, leaving the damp towel draped over a chair by the stove. Alex kept his hand over his crotch as he followed the naked man through the dark house to the stairs. Tucker slowly mounted the steps, his high, round butt inches from Alex as he followed behind.

Halfway up the steps, Tucker suddenly turned around. Alex felt the hot slap of the man's cock as it brushed across his face. He jerked his head back, his cheek burning from the contact and his breath catching in his throat.

"Oh, sorry," Tucker said quietly. "I forgot to get a glass of water."

"I'll get it," Alex stuttered and turned to run back into the kitchen. With shaking hands he poured out a glass of water from the pitcher and gulped it down, then paused to take a few deep breaths. He refilled the glass and, having regained a semblance of his composure but still sporting a rock-hard boner, ascended the steps, hoping against hope the room was dark enough to mask his condition.

When he entered the upstairs room he was relieved to find it illuminated only by the low light of the stove in the far corner as well as the waning light of the moon. Tucker hadn't lit any of the lanterns. He set the water glass on a table next to the side of the bed Tucker had claimed, the side Alex usually slept on, and rounded the end of the bed to sit carefully on the mattress.

Tucker raised his head and said over his shoulder, "Thanks for the water, Alex."

"You're welcome." He sat very still on the edge of the bed and stared out the window at the moonlit plains, trying to calm his fevered mind.

"Aren't you coming to bed?" The mattress pitched as Tucker rolled over to face him. "You must be pretty tired."

"Yeah, I am beat." He still hesitated. How could he possibly hope to sleep with this man lying buck naked beside him?

"Come on, buddy," Tucker coaxed, and turned back the covers. "The bed's warm. Take off your clothes and get in. You'll stay warmer if you sleep in the nude."

Alex pressed his lips together, knowing this was a deciding moment. A tension within him suddenly loosened and a sense of release spread through his chest as he took a breath and stood up. He pulled his arms from his long johns and let the underwear drop to the floor. After he stepped out of the garment, he pulled off his socks and kept his body turned away as he slid between the sheets. Tucker was right, the bed was warm. Or was it just his flush of sexual tension? Still nervous, he kept as close to the edge of the mattress as possible, his body rigid with anxiety. What if he had misinterpreted Tucker's intentions? How the hell would he get a moment's rest lying nude beside the man?

"Damn, you're tense." Tucker squeezed Alex's shoulder. "You need to relax."

Alex thought briefly, longingly, of his attempt to relax in the outhouse that morning. "Yeah, I do."

"How about if I help?" Tucker whispered, and reached across Alex's hip to take hold of his hard cock. Alex gasped as the man's fingers seared into the flesh of his cock. He'd never had another man's hand around him before. "Holy shit, buddy, you been sportin' that boner all day long?"

"Pretty much." Closing his eyes, Alex groaned and rolled onto his back as Tucker rubbed his throbbing cock.

"You must have a massive load saved up since this mornin' when I caught you pullin' your pud in the outhouse." Tucker's hot breath blew into Alex's ear as the man slid up against him. He felt the hot line of Tucker's own hardened cock press against his hip, and he groaned again. The whiskers of Tucker's beard scratched along his ear and the side of his face, and Alex shivered.

"You like my hand here?" Tucker asked.

"Yeah."

"You want to come like this?" Tucker slipped his tongue in Alex's ear and laughed when Alex jumped. "You want ol' Tucker to get you off?"

"Yeah, I do." Alex stretched his head back as Tucker increased the power and speed of his grip. "Oh, God! Yes, that's it. Right there at the top. Oh, yeah. Uh, uh, uh!" Alex felt his balls pull up, and then his mind soared above the plains outside the house as his seed spurted across his chin and throat. His eyes rolled back in his head, and he moaned his way down from the high of his orgasm, his mind slowly returning to its rightful place.

"Oh, my God," Alex gasped. Tucker's hand steadily slowed its strokes. The man's fingers squeezed more cum from the head of Alex's cock, sending another shiver through his spine.

"You sure got a lot of spunk in those balls." Tucker leaned over to run his tongue through the cum cooling on Alex's jaw. Alex turned his head and opened his mouth, taking Tucker's cum-covered tongue between his lips and sucking it clean.

Tucker rolled over to lie on top of Alex, their mouths tasting and caressing each other. Alex's cock hardened again and jabbed stiffly up into Tucker's stomach. The older man moved his mouth along Alex's hairy body, his tongue gliding through the puddles of drying cum and licking it up. He lightly bit each nipple, earning gasps and moans as he scraped his rough beard across the sensitive points of skin. He nuzzled into Alex's armpits and suckled the sweaty, soap-scented skin beneath the damp hair. Alex groaned and squirmed beneath Tucker's probing mouth.

Sliding lower, Tucker lapped up the cum that had puddled in Alex's navel, then made his way around the hard, red cock that stuck straight up along Alex's hairy belly to his large, heavy scrotum. He suckled each of the hairy balls nestled between Alex's muscular, furry legs, then ran his tongue along the shaft of the hard cock to its blunt head. Opening his mouth he took Alex all the way down his throat and began to suck him off.

"Oh, God!" Alex cried as Tucker swallowed him whole. He pressed his hands against the back of Tucker's head and bucked his hips.

Tucker adjusted himself, getting to his hands and knees over the younger man's groin as Alex pistoned his cock into Tucker's bearded face. Tucker increased the suction in his mouth and stroked his own rock-hard cock. Swinging his body around, he positioned his cock over Alex's face and let the full length of his shaft slap across the boy's cheeks. Alex immediately opened his mouth and took in the thick, hot cock, gagging as it filled his throat. Pulling back, he readied himself and raised his head again, taking it deep without choking as the foreskin slid back and the head poked the back of his throat.

Tucker withdrew Alex's cock from his mouth. "Easy with it," he coached. "Start off slow and work your way up along it."

Alex pulled Tucker's cock, wet with spit, from his mouth. "Okay." Holding the base tight in his fist, Alex took half of

Tucker's length down his throat. He pulled it out and slid the
glistening foreskin back from the tip. He smiled when the large,
pink head eased free of its cloak. He licked up the sweet precum
pooling at the slit, then released the foreskin and slid his tongue
beneath it.

"Oh, that's right, baby," Tucker groaned around his own
hot mouthful. "Get your tongue up under that foreskin. Oh, I
love that. You've done this before, haven't you?"

"Never," Alex replied, and opened wide to take Tucker completely into his mouth, gagging only slightly this time.

Tucker slipped his big hands beneath Alex's buttocks and
raised his hips, moving his tongue to the dark, damp tastes of
the younger man's ass. After running his tongue along the length
of Alex's crack, Tucker set to work licking and sucking at the
tightly puckered hole hidden beneath his dark body hair.

"Oh, Tucker," Alex groaned. "Oh, yes. Use your tongue."

Tucker slid his tongue deep inside Alex as he reached back to
stroke the slick, hard shaft he'd been sucking. Alex continued to
gobble down Tucker's cock as the man tightly rolled his tongue
and flicked it in and out of Alex's hole.

Tucker felt himself draw close to orgasm and just as his balls
tightened, he rose, kneeling alongside Alex's head and shoulders
with his cock stuffed straight down the younger man's throat.

"I'm going to come," Tucker cautioned. Alex moaned and
increased the force of his suction, bringing Tucker over the edge.
Tucker threw back his head and grunted, emptying his hot white
load into Alex. The spunk filled his mouth, and Alex guzzled
it down, savoring its heady, gamey taste. Pulling his cock free,
Tucker squeezed the last, thick drops out over Alex's open
mouth and leaned down to kiss him deeply. He sucked some of
his own juice from Alex's mouth, then licked around the man's
face and lapped up what remained from his stubbly cheeks.

"Did you like that?" Tucker asked.

"Yeah," Alex sighed.

They used their long johns to clean up and settled into bed beneath the heavy quilts. Tucker pulled Alex up close along his side and wrapped a big, beefy arm around him.

"Are you glad I interrupted you this morning?" Tucker asked sleepily.

"Oh, yeah," Alex said through a yawn. "Very glad."

They fell asleep as the moonlight glittered along the acres of Weston's Spread, the fingers of Alex's left hand tangled in the hair on Tucker's chest.

URBAN COWBOYS

Dominic Santi

Jake was what you might call an urban cowboy. He stood about five eight, slender and wiry, with close-cropped red hair and freckles. His idea of "business casual" was skintight faded denims, a pristine white T-shirt, cowboy boots, and a well-worn black Resistol that he tipped politely as he "sir"ed and "ma'am"ed his way down the hall to his cubicle each morning. It had been ten years since my last broken leg had forced me from the rodeo circuit and into an office, but I'd kept myself in shape, and I still appreciated young studs who wore the uniform comfortably and knew the value of a good horse.

This was Jake's first job since graduation. The other members of our equestrian supplies design team looked askance at the Western scenes on Jake's mouse pad. A couple of the snootiest were given to shuddering visibly at the country music blaring from his headphones when he tossed them on the desk and leaned his compact little ass back in his chair to chat. Personally,

I didn't give a fuck what Jake wore, or how he did his work. He was a helluva graphics artist, and he had a real feel for the needs and desires of both horses and the men who rode them. Hell, I even liked his taste in music.

I also knew his straight-guy routine was bullshit. As the MIS manager, I had unlimited access to the Internet-history files of all employees at the company. I snoop. Okay, I'm a shit—so sue me. I knew for a fact Jake spent damn near every lunch hour—and stayed late—using the company's ISDN lines to cruise some of the raunchiest gay porn sites on the Web. I sat up and took notice when he bookmarked some even I hadn't found yet. None of the VPs knew a mouse from their dick, so the information wasn't going anywhere—especially since I had records of the places those perverts visited, and the unlisted home phone numbers their wives answered.

A short while after finding out about Jake's predilections, I found myself again working late. The cubicles outside my glass-walled office were dark. So I drew the blinds and locked the doors. Then I went back to my desk and sat back down to admire the scenery.

Jake was kneeling on my desk, his ass in the air, jeans shoved down to his ankles and tangled around the tops of his boots. At my request, he wasn't wearing underwear. His hard-on bobbed just over the top of the polished mahogany, a clear strand of pre-cum drooling from the mostly exposed head of his surprisingly thick uncut dick. His lean, muscular thighs framed a couple of darkly furred, heavy low-hangers, and he'd been wiggling just enough that the toes of his boots had slipped over the edge of the desk, blocking access to the drawer. That was okay. I'd already put the condoms and a huge squirt-top bottle of lube next to my engraved penholder, which meant right next to where Jake's flushed face rested on his arms. His Resistol was perched on the middle of his back. I'd told him that if it fell off, I'd stop. He'd been squirming so much that I wondered if he hadn't glued the damn thing to his sweat-soaked tee.

Not that I had any intention of stopping. Without saying a word, I leaned forward and licked another long, slow swipe up my horny little rodeo pony's crack. He moaned into his arms and arched his ass back toward me. I obliged him by tickling my tongue over his pretty pink pucker.

"You like that, stud?"

"F-feels real good, Mr. B." Jake's hips twitched, and his asslips fluttered against my tongue.

"Tastes good, too," I laughed evilly. I reached down and resituated my hard-on, then put my palms on his asscheeks and deliberately drew them even farther apart. I swirled my tongue over his asslips. Jake groaned loudly. Gradually, I poked the tip in, reaching for his dank, tangy heat. As he loosened, I sank in enough to get a really good grip. Then I started sucking on his asslips.

"Fuck!" Jake bucked like a just-saddled colt. He arched into my mouth, moaning and clawing at the desk as I tongue-fucked him into fits. But the hat didn't fall off and he didn't try to get away. I'd learned real fast that Jake's not-so-straight asshole is the center of his universe. I slurped and sucked until his balls pulled up tight and I knew he was close to coming.

Then I leaned back and pressed a good-sized butt plug up his spit-slobbered ass. The toy slid in with damn near no resistance. Jake gasped and stiffened, his entire body going still as he realized what I'd done. Then he groaned and his ass commenced to clenching and flexing as he adjusted to the pressure of the firmly ensconced ass stretcher.

"Shit, Mr. B. That's big!"

Another large dollop of precum oozed out of his dick,

puddling on the shiny wooden desktop. I leaned back and admired the scenery, stroking my cock through my now-wet jeans and enjoying the smell of horny ass on my lips.

"It's just the right size to get you ready for mounting, ponyboy."

"Y-yes, sir," he gasped, breathing heavily as his ass muscles quivered. My little cowboy was adjusting to the feel of the thick horsehair tail hanging down from the base of the plug. I'd had it custom made, so the soft, brown, polyester faux hair was long enough to brush over the backs of his thighs if he wiggled just the right way. I watched Jake's hips work, trying to surreptitiously get the tail moving back and forth enough to tease the tops of his legs. Damn, that boy was a first-class slut.

"You make a damn fine ponyboy, Jake." I reached over and slapped his ass hard. "Keep that tail twitching so your cock and ass stay lively while I do some work."

To a muffled, "Yes, sir!" Jake's hips started a slow undulating motion, moving carefully from side to side. I wrapped one hand around my dick and took my mouse in the other. In reality, there was no way I was going to get any work done with a distraction like Jake at hand. But I knew he'd hear the clicks and beeps as I logged online and pulled up the main screen of what had turned out to be a favorite porn site for both of us. Jake would think I was ignoring him and nonchalantly working while he fought to take that thick, fake cock.

Fat chance of that, even though the models on the website were all cowboys. Lots of boots and hats and outdoor sucking and fucking in tranquil country scenes. None of the ass shots were anywhere near as good as what was waiting on my desk. In reality, I didn't want Jake squirming too much. His ass is so sensitive he'd eventually shoot just from that stimulation.

But I still wanted to play. He shivered as I pumped a huge

glob of lube into my hand. His groan seemed to vibrate through his whole body as I slathered the cool gel over his balls and started tugging.

"You're hung like a horse, pal. Think I'll help you work up a good load of sperm for me."

The horsehair brushed lightly over my arm, but Jake's overall movement slowed in response to the pressure on his nuts. I rubbed the heavy eggs between my fingers, savoring the warm fullness of his horny young flesh—and the way he jumped and gasped each time my thumb slid back to tease his perineum. With a final glance at the computer, I pumped out more lube and slicked up my own dick, shivering as the cool gel and my hot hand slid over my hungry horse dick.

"Looks like this particular ponyboy is hot to be fucked." My trail-boss voice wasn't particularly authentic, but I didn't give a shit. Apparently, Jake didn't either, from the way his cock jumped when I gloved it in my hand. I deliberately pulled his long, loose foreskin up over the glistening, deep red, hypersensitive head of his dick. He cried out, shaking as I jacked him, jacked us both, while the horsetail trailed over my arm.

I almost didn't stop in time. Jake stiffened. I grabbed the base of his dick hard, holding perfectly still and squeezing as I watched him shudder through a near-orgasm.

"No way, cowboy," I growled. "You don't get to come until this here stallion's dick is buried all the way up your slutty ass." When he nodded, I walked around to the other side of the desk and lifted my cock to his lips. "Get me ready to ride you, ponyboy. Get my big ol' stallion dick nice and slick so I can take you for a long, hard ride."

Jake licked once over the head, wetting it just enough for me to slide easily over his lips. Then he opened his throat. I gasped as he swallowed me whole. My nuts surged and I grabbed his ears, yanking him back and holding him still, closing my eyes so I wouldn't see his tongue reaching for me as I willed myself back from the edge. When I finally had my breathing under control again, I slapped his face sharply. Then I let him take me back in his mouth. Jake is the most enthusiastic cocksucker I've ever met. He purely loves to swallow dick. I panted through his rhythmic sucking as his tongue teased the hell out of the sensitive V beneath my dickhead.

"Mmm, boss. Damn, but you taste good!"

His hot tongue was fast as lightning, each jolt of searing licks followed by a long, wet, soothing slurp into his throat. I knew I couldn't take much of his talented mouth. So when my nuts were ready to explode, I thrust deep, one last time. Then leaned over him, and gave his ass a quick sharp slap. Jake's happy groan vibrated over my shaft as I pulled free of his dripping lips and went back around to his rear.

There was a puddle of precum beneath Jake's dick. His ass had been slowly rocking the entire time I fucked his throat. I grabbed his nuts again, squeezing them sharply a half-dozen times before I slowly stroked up his dick. Jake jumped so hard the hat lurched. With a devilish grin, I wiped the pool of cooling dick-juice onto my fingertips and slid my hand under his shirt. His tits were hard. They got harder as I pinched. Jake groaned and shivered.

"F-feels good, sir." The ass wiggle set the horsetail swinging again.

"Damn right," I growled, carefully hiding my shudder as the horsehair again tickled my arm. "I'm going to milk your tits and your dick and your nuts, then I'm going to fuck you, ponyboy." I twisted the other nipple. "This stallion's ready to mount your ass and ride you hard. You ready for some top-class stud service?"

"Yes, sir!" Jake gasped. He cried out as I pulled on the horsehair. I tugged a few more times, letting the plug stretch him some more. Then I slowly pulled the pony-tailed butt plug free. It was warm from his ass, slick and dripping with lube. His asslips were loose and puffy, so goddamn inviting. I couldn't resist one little kiss. Okay, more than one. Then I reached down and grabbed my dick. I indulged myself in a deep, long, slurping, sucking, tongue-fuck that had Jake moaning and shaking beneath me. Damn, his ass tasted fine.

"Please, sir. Please! Fuck, oh fuck! That feels good!"

My dick was ready to shoot. I stood up and gloved on the rubber. I stuffed handfuls of lube up Jake's ass and slathered my dick. Then I positioned myself, grabbed his slender hips, and let the tip of my dick kiss softly up against his waiting hole. As I pressed against the warm gate to his body, I licked my lips and once again savored the taste of Jake's ass.

"Get ready for a ride, cowboy," I growled, pressing in lightly. My dick slid in with no resistance. I shuddered as his warm, welcoming ass slowly enveloped my shaft. I swear his asslips kissed their way up my dick. Fuck, oh, FUCK! This boy was good! I held his hips tightly, setting up a slow, steady rhythm, in and out, in and out, grinding deep each time he gasped.

"Harder, sir. Fuck me harder. Right there! Please!"

I shook as he trembled violently at the pressure on his joy spot, then I shoved in again.

Jake's breathing quickened. I reached down and grabbed his nuts. They were tight up against his wildly waving cock. He was building up to one helluva come.

"These ready to shoot, cowboy? You ready to drain your balls with a good, hot come?"

"Yes, SIR!" he gasped. He arched up against me, the hat crushing between us. My hand slid down over his turgid shaft and as my fingers slid up, I felt the silky smoothness of his thoroughly exposed cockhead slide beneath my fingertips. Jake jerked hard beneath me. I felt the spasm all the way to my balls. I yanked his hips up hard and growled low in my throat.

"Jerk your dick, cowboy. We're going for a long, hard ride."

The ride was wild and rough. I ploughed his joy spot, bucking and grinding as the friction of his hole sliding over my shaft pulled the cum straight up out of my balls. I slid once more over his perfectly loosened asslips, sank deep into his hot, willing ass, then we yelled like banshees as Jake's asshole clamped down over my suddenly spurting dick. I rabbit-fucked him through a shattering orgasm that left him shaking in my arms and me hanging limply on his sweat-soaked back, nearly destroying his cowboy hat.

"Nice ass, stud," I laughed as I stood up, peeled off the rubber, and tossed it into the wastebasket. I gave his butt one more appreciative smack.

"Thanks, Mr. B.," Jake smiled sheepishly. He pushed up onto his arms and looked over his shoulder at me. "Um, I came all over your desk, sir."

He had. Buckets worth, it looked like. Ropes of his sperm stretched across the polished surface and some had splattered onto the lube bottle and my penholder. One long, white sticky glob dripped down the spine of my leather-bound dictionary. Definitely my kind of office decor, though I knew I'd have to clean it up before the custodial crews arrived.

"Same time next week, Mr. B.?"

"You bet your ass," I laughed, yanking my pants back up and tucking my thoroughly contented dick back inside.

"I did," he grinned. As he spoke, he stood up, pulling up his jeans and slowly turning around. The squashed Resistol stayed in place in the middle of his back. As I started to laugh, he grinned unrepentantly.

"I stapled it to my shirt this time, sir. But I'm real good at designing ways to keep people in the saddle. You'll see."

I had. And I fully intended to see more. I wiped down my desk, threw the toys in my bottom desk drawer, and pressed the lock. Then I followed Jake out the door and killed the lights.

Damn, I love my job.

PANIOLO

Neil Plakcy

"Of course, when I wear these chaps at a rodeo, I've got jeans on underneath," Kalani said, modeling them for me with nothing else on. "What do you think, Kimo?"

"I like them better like this," I said. He was shirtless, and as I reached up and rubbed his nipples, his dick stiffened and stuck out of the opening at his crotch at a forty-five-degree angle. I kissed him, and our tongues danced with each other, the way Kalani and I had two-stepped earlier that night.

Kalani was the handsomest, sexiest cowboy at the Paniolo Festival, and when I saw him that morning astride his palomino, I knew that if he turned out to like guys as much as I did, I wanted to ride that cowboy.

Almost any Hawaiian is proud to tell you that the paniolos were the first American cowboys. Captain George Vancouver brought the first cows to Hawaii in 1792, and the first horses arrived around 1804. In 1832, Hawaii's king invited Mexican vaqueros to teach islanders how to rope and ride. Because these wranglers spoke Spanish, the Hawaiians corrupted the word *español* into *paniolo*, and the word came to mean "Hawaiian cowboy." Mainland cowboys only date to the 1870s, when vaqueros from Mexico started teaching Texans to ride and rope.

The Paniolo Festival celebrates the heritage of our island cowboys. You might think Hawaii is all palm trees, beaches, and volcanoes, but the Parker Ranch, the largest privately owned ranch in the United States, is on the Big Island. As a mixed-race kid, part Hawaiian, part Japanese, and part haole (white), I'd grown up on legends of the paniolos—playing either the cowboys or the Indian—and my favorite part of the game was when Georgie Kamura tackled me and took me prisoner inside his makeshift wigwam. For some reason he insisted I remove all my clothes before he tied me up, but I didn't mind one bit.

I guess I was remembering those childhood games when I decided to fly to the Big Island for the Paniolo Festival. I lost touch with Georgie in seventh grade, when my parents sent me to private school, but I was hoping I might find a new cowboy to play with. Plus, something about all those sexy cowboys in one place really made my dick stand up and salute.

It's only a forty-minute flight from Honolulu to Kona, on the Big Island, so I flew out early Saturday morning, picked up a rental car at the airport, then drove to the festival. I'd taken some care in getting dressed, wearing a Chicago Homicide T-shirt that read, OUR DAY STARTS WHEN YOURS ENDS, a tight pair of jeans that accented my butt, and worn cowboy boots.

I watched the parade, noting Kalani James as he pranced by me on his palomino pony. He wore jeans and a light-blue chambray shirt, scuffed brown cowboy boots, and a bright red lei of scarlet lehua flowers. He had a shock of dark hair, a killer smile, and biceps that rippled as he shook the palomino's reins. He looked my way. Our eyes locked for a moment, and I felt little electric shocks go shooting through my body.

A little later I watched Kalani come in first in the quarter-mile race, and snapped a digital picture of him accepting his award. After he stepped down from the dais, I made a point of meeting up with him. "Hey," I said, reaching out to shake his hand. "You rode a great race."

"Thanks," he said. Our eyes locked again, and he smiled. We introduced ourselves, and I used the display on the back of my camera to show him the picture I'd taken. "Hey, that's great," he said. "I'd love to get a copy of that."

I offered to email him one, but he said, "I've got a computer at my place. Maybe you could stop by and download it."

From the glint in his eye I could tell the picture wasn't the only thing he was interested in. "Sure," I said.

He looked at his watch. "I've got to be back here at four for the roping competition. But I've got a couple of hours free. If you'd like to..."

"Sure," I said. "I've got a car in the lot."

He shook his head. "Pua's faster," he said, "for where we're going." Pua, which means flower in Hawaiian, was his palomino's name. I followed him to where he'd tied her up. In a quick motion he'd jumped onto her back then gestured for me to follow.

I wasn't quite so graceful, but I got up behind him. "Give me your hands," he said over his shoulder, and I began to reach around his waist. He took my hands and placed them firmly around his waist. "You just hold on tight."

I scooted up so that my dick was right up against his ass, and he shook the reins. Pua took off at a trot until we cleared the festival grounds. With another shake and a little action in her flanks, she picked up the pace.

Kalani was warm and sexy, and a mixture of his sweat and aftershave filled my nostrils. My dick loved the friction of riding up against his ass, but my butt was bouncing along like a dribbled basketball, and I was deathly afraid of losing my grip on Kalani and sliding backward over Pua's tailbone.

We cantered up a slope, then down a country road. Ten minutes later Kalani was reining Pua in as we approached a doublewide trailer on a gorgeous piece of countryside. "It's not much, but it's home," he said. As we came to a stop, I loosened my death grip on his waist, and he jumped off, saying, "I liked it when you were holding on to me. You're gonna have to do that again real soon."

I tried to get off the horse as gracefully as he had, but I ended up stumbling and sliding off and right into Kalani's arms—which come to think of it, was just where I wanted to be. We kissed for the first time then, under the warm sun, with Pua breathing heavily next to us.

The kiss was tentative at first, just our lips meeting, but as I wrapped my arms around him and felt out bodies mesh together, our lips opened. His face was a little sandy against mine, but the scrape of his light beard only incited me to kiss him more deeply. I was conscious of the twenty places were our bodies touched each other; the way his hand rested lightly on my shoulder blade; the warm pulse of his living, breathing dick against my leg.

Finally, Kalani pulled back. "Come on, let me show you what's inside." He took my hand and led me into the trailer. "I'll skip most of the tour for right now." He led me through a door to the right, into a bedroom with a double bed under a bright-red Hawaiian quilt.

"More scarlet lehua," I said, before Kalani turned and started kissing me again.

The next few minutes were a frantic blur, both of us struggling to get out of our clothes as quickly as possible while not breaking the kiss. We fell onto the bed with our pants around our ankles, both of us stuck in cowboy boots that wouldn't come off so easily. But it didn't matter—we rolled around on the bed together, our stiff dicks rubbing against each other as we kissed and panted for breath.

I'm a strong guy; I don't really work out, but I surf, run, and Rollerblade, and I've got a pretty good body. Kalani was an equal match for me—six-pack abs, ropy biceps, and strong calves and thighs, from all that riding. His body was smooth, like mine, with a dusting of chest hair, tufts under his arms, and a wiry black thatch around his groin. He had a dolphin tattoo on his back, just above his buttcrack, and a thin, wavy scar around one kneecap.

Finally, Kalani pulled off and scooted down the bed a bit to take my dick in his mouth. I was so worked up that almost as soon as his warm lips touched my stiff rod, I knew I would come. I warned him, and he pulled back, finishing me off with his hand as I spurted up over his fist.

He flipped over onto his back, and I got to work on his dick, licking it from top to bottom, tonguing the piss-slit, then deep-throating him. His body tensed, and he made whimpering sounds—my cue to finish him off with my hand the way he'd done for me.

Then there we were, lying next to each other on the bed, both of us catching our breath, both with a handful of cum and jeans twisted around our cowboy boots. "Man, that was hot," he said, finally. "We both went off like rockets on the Fourth of July." With his free hand he pulled his pants up a bit, hopped off the bed, and walked across to the bathroom. I did the same.

After our hands were clean, we were able to disentangle our

jeans and boots. A warm breeze wafted through the open windows of the trailer, caressing our bodies as we lay next to each other. We traded life stories then. I told him I was a homicide cop in Honolulu, and he explained that he was a carpenter during the week and a rodeo cowboy whenever he could be.

Pretty soon he looked at the clock. "I've got to get back for the roping," he said. "Will you stick around?"

"I've got a ticket for the last flight out tonight, but I can change it to tomorrow." A deep kiss and a quick caress from my crotch to my chest told me he was happy with that idea.

We rode back to the festival together, and this time I was able to get off Pua's back without falling, before Kalani cantered off to the roping competition. His team was slow, though, and didn't win anything—which was just fine with me, because it meant he was back at my side that much sooner.

We walked around the festival together for a while then ended up at the two-step dance. We joined the men's line next to each other, and it was fun trying to match my rhythm to his.

"Come on," he said, when a song—probably the fifth or sixth—ended. "Let's get something to eat then head back to my place."

There was a huge luau at one end of the festival grounds, and we ate our fill of kalua pig, chicken long rice, poi, shark-fin soup, sweet and sour spareribs, and Portuguese sausage and beans. Though my stomach was groaning, we had to have dessert: pineapple, banana, and mango ice cream. Finally, when neither of us could eat another bite, Kalani said, "I'll ride Pua back to my place—on the road, this time, and you can follow in your rental car."

Driving up to his trailer, I started yawning. Too much excitement, too much food, I thought. Would I be able to get it up again, or would I fall asleep as soon as my body hit that double bed? I must have dawdled a bit, because Kalani disappeared inside the trailer, then reappeared a couple of minutes later wearing only his chaps.

I walked up to where he stood in the doorway of the trailer and kissed him. I was about to drop to my knees and take his dick in my mouth when he said, "Come inside, cowboy. And this time take off your boots."

I followed him to the bedroom, and he sat back on the bed in his chaps and watched me strip. I was hard even before I got my boots off—just seeing his lean, muscular chest; the leather chaps with their big round opening; and of course his sleek, hard dick staring at me. Though I felt my blood rush, I tried to take it slow—what good is having a killer body if you can't show it off sometimes? I teased and tantalized him a bit, exposing first one nipple then the other, then taking off my shirt. I unbuttoned my jeans and let them sag open, giving him a glimpse of pubic hair, then turned my back to him and eased them over my butt, sliding my boxers down with them.

I looked at Kalani over my shoulder as my pants dropped to the floor and I stepped out of them. "Man, you've got a great ass," he said. "Come here and sit on my dick."

"You want me to ride you, cowboy?"

He reached for the bedside table and then ripped open a condom, which he slid over his stiff dick. He squeezed some lube into his hand and rubbed it up and down his pole, all the while staring into my eyes.

I couldn't resist any longer. I climbed onto his bed and positioned my ass in front of him. "Grease me up, boy. I'm ready to ride."

The lube was cool, but as his finger worked it up my ass it warmed. When he pulled out his finger, I squatted over his dick and lowered myself onto him. It hurt a bit at first, but I went slow. Once my ass was accustomed to him, I moved up and down, faster, building a rhythm. My calves locked onto his around the leather chaps, and my thighs strained, but I didn't pay them any attention—I was focused on the sweet feeling of his dick riding in and out of my ass, clenching my muscles around him, moving faster and faster as he made those little moaning noises again.

He was really crying out by the time I felt him release into me. I slid off his dick after he stopped panting, and lay there next to him. "Somebody's still hard as a rock," he said, reaching over to stroke my dick. "We're gonna have to do something about that."

Kalani ripped open another condom and slid it over me, then rubbed lube over me with a gentle, almost feathery movement. I worried I'd come again fast if he kept that up, but he didn't. Instead he stood and moved over to the bureau, which he grasped with both hands. Then he bent over. The chaps cupped his ass, leaving it open for me like a special present on Christmas morning.

I squeezed some lube onto my finger, but before I stuck it up his ass I bent down to give him a tongue bath, gripping the sides of the leather chaps. In and out my tongue shot, loosening his muscles and making him squirm again. "Oh, man, stop teasing me," he said at last. "Fuck me. Stick your dick up my ass *now*."

As I said, I'm a cop, and our motto is "Serving and Protecting with Aloha." It was time for me start serving, and I did—I served my dick right up his tight slippery ass. He was whimpering again, but I didn't know if it was pain or pleasure, and I didn't care. I drove my dick up his ass until my nuts banged against his skin then pulled almost all the way out and drove it in again. I braced my hands against his shoulders and plowed him until my whole body erupted with the force of my orgasm.

Suddenly I could barely stand. It was all I could do to pull out of his ass and stumble to the bed. "You all right?" he asked, looking over.

"You killed me." I moved my hand over my heart. "Fucked to death. But man, what a way to go."

Kalani laughed and jumped on top of me, and we wrestled for a while. Finally, we settled in for the night, spooned against each other, his limp dick nestling in the curve of my ass. I hoped he didn't have anything planned for Sunday, because I'd booked myself on the last flight back to Honolulu, and I knew I wanted to try those chaps on myself.

FACING THE MATADOR

CB Potts

I hadn't wanted to spend Saturday afternoon fixing fence, but that damn bull had broken out again. I couldn't really blame Diablo. The poor bastard was hell-bent on getting some tail, and there was precious little of that in his corral.

Every chance he got, he'd push down the fence and head down the road to the Bar S. I'd have to once again round up a few reluctant assistants, clamber into the pickup, and try to retrieve him—not easy when he was in the throes of love with some comely heifer.

Of course, I could build better a fence—confine my wayward stud with the latest in barbwire technology, coupled with the stinging shock only electric fencing can provide. But that would be expensive—and it would probably keep Diablo in. And if that happened, when would I get to see Marco?

Marco had been at the Bar S for three years, and for every day of those three years, I had lusted after him. When I closed my eyes at night, I saw the long, brown curves of his body—I heard the musical lilt his accent lent to the most prosaic of sentences. Under the guise of an interested ranch owner, always looking for more hands, I'd found out everything I could about Marco. I knew he was quiet, that he kept to himself. I knew he could ride a horse like nobody's business and that he had a way with animals that was a marvel to behold.

What I didn't know was Marco's secret history. My first clue of his previous identity came on yet another bull-retrieving mission. Sure, it was a pain in the ass, but it's also important to remember that an irate bull is a few hundred pounds of hoofed death. I'd never had Diablo's horns polled, so with one good swipe of the head my bull could disembowel a careless cowboy. One didn't tangle lightly with a critter like that!

I hadn't discovered Diablo's latest escape until late in the evening, when I was going out to the barn to retrieve a forgotten T-shirt. Bachelor or no, sometimes you've just got to do laundry. Walking through the twilight, I turned to greet my prize stud and found the corral empty.

"Son of a bitch!" I cursed. It was payday, and most of the hands were off on their weekly drinking binge. If I wanted to get Diablo, I was on my own. To top it all off, the crew had taken the truck with them.

It was a few miles to the Bar S, and by the time I'd arrived, the moon shone brightly. The light allowed me to spot Diablo right away—and to let me see he wasn't alone.

Usually a bull with loving on his mind does nothing else, but Diablo was acting funny. He was circling the pasture, occasionally darting toward the middle and then away, his churning hooves pounding clouds of dust up to heaven.

Trying to figure it out, I edged closer. That's when I saw Marco, standing in the middle of Diablo's vision and holding a red T-shirt. He'd snap that garment, drawing Diablo back to him time after time, taunting the raging bull. Each time, Diablo charged, and each time, at the last possible moment, Marco moved inches out of his path. I couldn't count the times flashing horns barely missed Marco's tender abdomen, couldn't number how often Death almost collected the sexy ranch hand.

Despite the terror of the situation, the life-or-death choices every second held for Marco, I found I couldn't interfere, couldn't turn away. It would only take one shout, one quick loop of the rope, and this whole scene would stop. Instead I stood, eyes riveted to the scene, my prick growing uncomfortably hard inside my jeans.

Frustrated, Diablo pawed the ground. His head lowered until his snout brushed the sage grass. Marco shifted his hips, eyes locked with the raging bull. For an eternal moment they just stared.

Then Diablo charged. With nearly a ton of angry beef bearing down on him, Marco didn't move a muscle. He didn't even blink. The distance between them closed until it was ten feet, five feet, two feet, one...

And then Marco vaulted into the air, twisting his body to narrowly avoid Diablo's deadly horns. He had the grace of a gymnast combined with the skill of the finest rodeo performer. He landed behind Diablo and gave the puzzled bull a smack on the flank.

Frustrated yet again, the bull left in search of easier conquests. I left the safety of the fence and stood inches from Marco.

"You know that's fucking nuts, what you just did," I raged. "You could have been killed."

Marco laughed, teeth glinting in the moonlight. "Not today, my friend, not today." His smile deepened. "Sometimes you have to take risks. It's a rush to get what you want."

"Is that what you want?" I countered, exasperated. "To be gored by my bull?"

"Not by your bull, perhaps," Marco replied. His gaze dropped to my bulging jeans. "But something else could be interesting."

My mouth went dry, and my legs turned to jelly.

"What do you mean?" I stammered. Could the object of my fantasies actually be interested in me?

My answer came soon enough, as Marco's fingers undid my belt. He slid his hand inside, wrapping around my rock-hard prick.

"What do you think I mean?" he asked. "Do you have any ideas?"

I nodded, silent with desire.

Marco smiled. "That's what I thought you'd say." Before I knew what was happening, the hot ranch hand pulled my pants down till they were bunched around my boots, wrapped my rod in a thin coat of latex, and slid those sexy lips down to my balls.

"Sweet Jesus!" I breathed. My prick raged inside Marco's talented mouth. His tongue did tricks I didn't know were possible—circling my tool like a constricting snake, squeezing an already overstimulated organ.

I slid back and forth, trying to stuff even more down Marco's throat. At first he took it willingly, but after a few of my enthusiastic thrusts, he gripped my hips. The forced slowing of the pace made each moment more enjoyable, and I felt my juices about to erupt.

"I'm gonna come," I announced, not caring who heard me. "Come in your mouth."

"No." Marco quickly pulled his head away. "You're gonna come in my ass."

I reached for his blue-black hair, intending to draw his talented mouth back to business. "I can do both."

"I've only got one skin, man—and I want you in my ass!"

Well, when the choice was put like that, it was easy to decide. I hadn't thought to bring any condoms with me, and who knew when this opportunity would come again.

Marco stood before me. I waited for half a heartbeat, then realized he wanted me to take some initiative. It's very different to undo someone else's belt, but I managed. Marco wore his jeans much tighter than I did, and I had to peel them away from his muscular thighs. There's no better scent than that of a horny man, sweaty from exertion and hungry for more.

When Marco's prick sprang free, it reared upward, almost slapping his stomach in its eagerness. It was a long shaft, nearly nine inches, capped with the purplest head I've ever seen. There was no way to keep my hands off it.

Used to my own thickness, I was surprised that my fingers completely encircled Marco's meat. A few gentle strokes had the ranch hand moaning in a stream of Spanish. I spat into my hand, making sure my palm was slick with saliva. Then I gripped Marco's prick and jacked him off.

"Tighter," he hissed, and I squeezed. My own prick, raging hard but forgotten in the heat of the moment, bumped against Marco's asscheeks. I slowly rubbed over that tan, hairless plain, matching each stroke to the rhythm of my hand on Marco's prick.

"Faster," he commanded, and I quickly obliged. His prick writhed in my hand, passion about to erupt, when he abruptly pushed his ass back at me.

"Now," he said. "Fuck me now!"

Pushing slowly into Marco's ass, I discovered new meanings for *hot* and *tight*. The way his sphincter snapped around my head, you'd think I was going in there for keeps.

Each inch inward was an exquisite struggle, as Marco's ass

muscles gripped me in ways I hadn't thought possible. The pressure exerted in his hot little chute more than doubled the pleasure I'd found in his mouth.

A strange motion at the edge of my vision caught my attention, and I turned to see Diablo mounting a willing cow. *Good for you, old friend,* I thought, sliding farther into Marco's ass. *If what you're getting is half as good as what I'm getting, I'd be knocking down fences, too.*

Marco grunted deeply. "Am I hurting you?" I asked, slowing my motion to a standstill.

"No," he moaned. "Don't stop...I'm gonna come any second now."

"Don't come until I'm all the way in you," I pleaded. There was no way I was going to miss feeling the convulsions inside Marco's glory hole while he was shooting off.

"Then give it to me fast!" Marco panted.

My hips arched forward, trying to gently force the last few inches into an already overstuffed cavern. It would have been possible, I suppose, to brutally push the rest of my manhood in, but I didn't want to hurt him. Chances were I'd never get to tangle with him again if I screwed up now.

So I wound up not quite entirely inside Marco when I felt his hot juice explode all over my busy hand. His entire body went limp with the force of his orgasm, and if it weren't for my prick buried deep inside his ass, I'm sure the cowboy would have crumpled to the ground.

Marco's ass muscles tensed so tightly when he came, I was sure he'd bruise my prick. But despite the slight pain, the combined pleasure of watching Marco climax, hearing his Spanish prayers to heaven, and feeling the incredible heat inside his chute was making it high time for me to unleash my own load.

"Here it comes," I announced. My sticky hands left Marco's

prick to glue themselves to his narrow hips. Each stroke came faster and faster, went deeper and deeper. "I'm gonna come in your ass just like you wanted."

"Just like I wanted," Marco echoed. Somehow he managed to make his ass even tighter, as he reached around to grab at me, trying to pull me deeper inside his hungry hole.

Just then I exploded, feeling the condom swell with my hot load. It's a good thing I had a grip on the base, or Marco's hungry ass would have swallowed it whole when it started to slip.

Afterward, we stood, dressing ourselves in the still moonlight. Diablo had finished his business and was placidly munching clover not fifteen feet from us.

"Think he enjoyed the show?" I asked,

"Maybe," Marco replied. "He's a good bull—the type I used to fight in Spain." He grinned, white teeth flashing in the moonlight. "That's the dream I thought I would have forever, you know?"

"So what happened?"

"Over there, I got caught being gored by the wrong kind of bull, you know? They don't put up with that—I had to leave. Over here," Marco smiled, boldly running his eyes over me, "no one cares what kind of horns stick you."

SECRETS OF THE GWANGI

Steve Berman

Tuck Kirben had never hidden from danger once in his thirty-four years—not when he outrode a wild twister in the Kansas territory, not when that crazed Chinaman with the hatchet had wanted to settle a gambling score, and certainly not when an entire saloon full of men had been ready to lynch him after learning what he'd done on the piano the very night before. But damn it, he now found himself hiding underneath a rock outcropping like a snake without its rattle and with only half a fang.

From where he crouched, he couldn't see any of the *gwangi*, as T. J. called the fucking things, but Tuck knew they soared above, just waiting to pick him off like he was some scampering jackrabbit. Sweat rolled down Tuck's body, and his unbuttoned soiled shirt stuck to his chest and back like a second skin. Even as the sun set, the jungle valley held the heat like scorched Texas dirt. He cursed that map that had promised silver veins as thick as a man's arm; if there was any ore down here, he doubted they'd ever live to find it. He wiped his brow beneath his wide-brimmed hat. Salt stung his eyes and sweat dripped onto the coarse paper, as he scribbled in his journal. That old school-marm who'd done taught him letters would be all hobbled if she ever read his words.

He heard the crunch of gravel from behind him, reached for his pistol and nearly shot poor T. J. full of lead. He offered the vaquero a sorry grin of apology. Tuck had traveled down to Mexico looking to challenge the infamous Tiago Josue Sanz to a gunfight. He had found the man holding court in a vast cantina. T. J. had pushed the painted whore off his knee and accepted the challenge. But first tequila. Though he'd been bottle sharp since knee high, Tuck had never drunk so much in all his days, matching the dreadfully handsome tawny-skinned devil glass for glass. Finally, somewhere between toasts to *el de atras* and *ir a un entierro*, Tuck had found himself wanting more to fuck T. J. than shoot him. The vaquero had eyes like Spanish mission-ary chocolate, and his carefully groomed mustache ached to be messed by fierce lips. The painted stripe, red like fire, running down T. J.'s tight pants had taunted Tuck.

When they had stumbled out of the cantina together, full as ticks, trying to walk and too stubborn to collapse, Tuck half dragged, half sweet-talked the Mexican man back to the edge of town. Behind some sagebrush he fought him to the ground. No six-shooters were needed, only the red-hot iron unshucked from his opponent's wool pants. He tasted every inch of T. J., sucked down his *mecos* like it was marrow and he was a starving man. The stuff was fine as creamy gravy on Tuck's tongue. He made sure T. J. knew he could break any bronco, especially one who cussed as he moaned.

Afterward, well, there weren't any need for the gunfight. He stayed in town for a while 'til T. J.'s amigos began whispering and giving him steel glares. Tuck had been ready to silence them quick, but by then T. J. had found the old prospector's body and the map.

Shit, Tuck wished they'd never gone off looking for silver. Taking on a dozen thick-headed south-of-the-border hounds would be a heap better than battling these giant flying lizard-vultures.

"I scouted the area. Counted four in the sky." T. J. pulled off his sarape. His thick dark hair remained askew, and Tuck gently cleared the vaquero's forehead, which felt feverish. There weren't much water left in their canteens and only crumbs in their packs.

The *gwangi* ate proper on their horses. Tuck didn't think there'd be anything left of poor Stokes and Tana than cracked bones and iron shoes. He needed to find them some water to cool off in and drink. It would bring T. J.'s fever down. Then they could think straight and figure a way to get out.

Willis put down the yellowed sheets of paper gently, but a curled edge still broke loose on his workshop desk. He took out a handkerchief from his pocket and absently wiped his fingers clean.

"Genuine?"

The Mexican fellow, who'd been staring at the various armatures and half-made puppets, swung his head back to face Willis and nodded, almost violently, while beginning a chanted barrage of "Yes" and "*Sí.*" He nervously clutched the battered leather satchel that had kept the journal safe for almost a century.

Willis took out his wallet. The act silenced the Mexican man, and his eyes grew wide, no doubt in anticipation. Just how long after his phone call had he been waiting for some gringo to count out bills?

The story of the century only cost Willis eighty-three dollars.

Or the greatest hoax. Not that it mattered. What was making movies but a combination of both?

Tuck offered the last of his water to T. J. Together, their fingers held the canteen. He fought the urge to kiss away the drops that hung on T. J.'s lips and mustache. Now weren't the time for such things.

He cautiously looked out at the sky from underneath the rock. Plenty of clouds in the clear blue, but it looked anything but calm. Any one of those clouds could be hiding a hungry *gwangi*.

Still, they had to move while there was light. At night they could stumble through the jungle and miss a pond three feet from them. Tuck put away his journal. He hoped he'd have a chance to write more later. In one hand he held his shooting iron; with the other he took hold of T. J.'s sweaty palm.

Willis arrived early for his meeting with the studio executive. He paced near the receptionist who watched him warily out of the corner of her eye. Her fingers went *clickety-clack* on the typewriter keys. Normally, the sound comforted him—he always considered it a cunning echo of creative energy—but that afternoon he found the typing an uncomfortable staccato. He tried not to glare at her, worried she might think he was staring at the more-than-ample tits straining her fuzzy blouse.

The phone rang, and in one smooth motion the receptionist swept the receiver up to her ear. "Yes, sir," she said. When she told Willis he could go in she didn't even look at him.

The studio executive's office had its own personal fog bank, not Thames murk but Chesterfield bluish-gray smoke drifting about the ceiling. Willis had never known the man to have a hand or mouth empty of a cigarette.

"Thank you for seeing me—"

"Willis, are you trying to give me a heart attack?" The executive leaned back and stabbed at the front of his vest. Ashes flickered about his person.

"I don't understand."

"This *dreck*." The man slid a thick yellowed hand over the pages on his immense mahogany desk and sent them cascading over the edge in a magnificent paper waterfall into the wastebasket. "*The Valley Time Forgot.* Pfeh. I wish I could forget I read it."

"It's the queer thing, right? But this," Willis said, lifting up his own copy of the screenplay that represented thirteen days of sweat and blood spent over the keys of his Remington, his thoughts consumed with imaging how metal wire and papiermâché could bring the creatures to life. "This is guaranteed drive-in gold."

"You're fucking nuts, Willis, if you think anyone wants to see a movie about two faggot cowboys—"

"What about the ferocious pterodactyls?"

"More dinosaurs and less *faygelehs*. That's what makes a movie." The executive flicked open his gilded lighter, even though his last cigarette still smoldered at the corner of his mouth.

Thirteen years after the filming wrapped, the drive-ins of suburban New Jersey have gone the way of the dinosaur. UHF features all the horror and fantastical films on Saturday and Sunday afternoons. Steve sits on the floor in the den, his friend Chucky close by, and watches the movie on the bulky console RCA television.

Steve holds one of the couch pillows in his lap, almost as if hiding behind it. Not that the monsters on the seventeen-inch screen are the least bit threatening, but lately he finds Chucky to be so. Or rather, his thoughts about Chucky. He turns back to the television and decides the movie would be a lot cooler if the handsome cowboy—who has the silly name of Tuck, which must have been just awful when the guy went to school—wouldn't bother so much with the girl. Yeah, Steve thinks, grabbing a handful of Fritos from the bowl by Chucky's knees, T. J. ought to have been a guy. Then the kissing part wouldn't be so bad. Not that Steve has ever kissed another boy, but he does wonder a lot about it, especially when he's around Chucky.

On the curved glass screen the cowboys begin to lasso the clay allosaurus. Chucky starts to laugh. His breath reeks of corn chips. "That's so gay."

Steve winces, and then, with a steadiness that surprises him, lifts a hand up in a pistol gesture. He takes aim at Chucky's handsome features and clicks his thumb. Bang.

On the makeshift studio lot the dust settled to the earth minutes after the jeep stopped. Esteban looked over his shoulder and saw the loco American leap from where he had sat in the back, still clutching some sort of pole. Esteban didn't understand why he had to drive around in circles while men tried to rope the pole's end. But the movie business paid well.

In the passenger seat, Carlos laughed as the movie folk scrambled like busy ants. Esteban loved the sound of Carlos's deep laughter as it so often came before an embrace. Making sure no one watched, he reached over and firmly squeezed the crotch of his friend's denim jeans.

Carlos favored him with a smile.

"Tonight," Esteban said, leaning in close, "let's steal away to the jungle set and pretend we are lost in their valley."

"What of the monsters?" The crazy American who had

wielded the pole played with toy lizards, posing them for hours.

Esteban squeezed more and felt the reassuring firmness and heat beneath his palm. "I like some monsters." He kissed Carlos, tasting a bit of the road dirt in the man's mouth, but the grit did not last long. "Besides, we can play cowboy." He made sure to say the word in English, feeling it strange and wondrous on his lips.

THE NEW SHERIFF

Dale Chase

In April 1864, when I last rode to Springfield, Edgar Rawlings had been sheriff. I knew him to be an honest man possessed of a quick gun hand, but his skill did him little good as he was ambushed soon after arresting Bob Brown. It was believed Bob's brother Ben pulled the trigger, but nobody was saying and the deputy had made himself scarce. Now, six months later, I was back in town.

"New man coming," a bartender said after I remarked on the absence of a sheriff.

"And we still got laws," insisted a drunken cowboy, but then another laughed. "Who's to enforce them?" the man said. "You wanna put on a badge and go after Ben Brown?"

No reply came, and I turned to watch cowhands doing their drinking and gambling; whatever coin remained after these pursuits was destined for the whores upstairs. I stayed by the bar, hoping to see the blacksmith's assistant, a man I fucked whenever I got to town.

"Clay Carver? You ain't heard? Gunned down two weeks ago," I was told when I asked after him.

I swear I felt the bullet myself, tearing through me and leaving a deep wound. Clay was a good man, honest, straightforward, never giving anyone a lick of trouble. But he fucked men, and without so much being said, I knew that might be the reason his life had been taken.

"Had him some trouble down at the livery," a grizzled man said with a whiskey leer. I knew he wanted me to ask more so his cock could grow hard as he told. He knew about Clay and was guessing about me, so I offered nothing more and changed the subject.

"Who's the new sheriff?" I asked him.

"Man named Alden Reed, due to arrive next week. He's known to be hard, much experienced, with little tolerance for lawlessness. Word is Ben Brown has moved on."

"Alden Reed?"

"Out of Wichita."

I'd never heard of him, but I missed a lot of what went on as I worked on a ranch some distance away and only came to town when I got my monthly pay. It was then I'd see Clay at the livery or the saloon and we'd meet after dark and fuck. My cock stirred at the thought of him even though he was dead, so I forced my mind toward the new sheriff. Maybe he was man enough to bring in Clay's killer.

In the days before his arrival, talk of Reed grew. The idea of him aroused me much the way Clay had, and I envisioned a big thick man with a good-sized cock. Of course I took the idea beyond what others did, wondering if he might like men instead of women. I reminded myself this wasn't likely his persuasion but decided there was no reason not to enjoy the pleasures of speculation. So as I lay in my hotel room working my swollen prick, I let my mind consider.

I saw him push an unruly drifter to his knees, saw the sheriff unbutton his pants and take out his prick, shove it into the waiting mouth, thrusting as the man gagged. I saw the gun belt slung across the sheriff's hip, the cock below taking what it needed. I heard the drifter's cry as the sheriff let go his spunk and made the man swallow, holding him there on the prick, and when the sheriff pulled out he was still erect, the big thing dripping with his juice. I saw him then make the drifter strip, get down like a pony, saw the pecker go up the man's bottom and ride out another come. I would've pictured more except I began to squirt and pumped my rod as pleasure ran through me.

Of course I had it all wrong about the sheriff, at least with his looks. It's always a mistake to anticipate, as reality is seldom as you want to see it. Still, he was impressive. Tall and lean, he bore the hard look people had said, weathered by the sun, lined by life. His hair was black; his mustache gray, a clue to his age. Quick and sure in his step, he was rumored to have the reflexes of a cat. He said little, speaking with action rather than words. A few days after he arrived, he brought in a haggard Ben Brown, reduced to sullenness. None would say how the capture had come about.

I made the sheriff's acquaintance when a scuffle occurred in the saloon and I was drawn in. Though people in town knew I fucked men, it wasn't discussed. Most allowed me my privacy. Certain things were tolerated so long as they were not done openly, but that day in the bar, an itinerant preacher scorned my conversation with another cowhand I had fucked in the past. When the preacher started in, the cowhand hit him in defense of me, and I was grabbed and wrestled to the floor. When the sheriff stepped in he took us all to the jailhouse where things were sorted out.

He released the preacher and cowhand but kept me on, leaning against his desk while I sat before him. As he spoke I noted the bulge at his crotch, a sizeable thickening that ran down his thigh. I quickly lost track of our talk as I was greatly in need. A week in town and no fucking. I was tired of my own hand, eager for cock. And Sheriff Reed knew it.

As he spoke about the incident at the saloon his hand came to rest on his bulge and he rubbed himself. "People like that preacher don't want to understand about men. I'd reckon his anger about what you might do with another man is fueled partly by his Bible-reading and partly by his desire to do the very thing he condemns."

The sheriff began to unbutton his pants, pulling them open below the gun belt, talking all the while. "Preacher up in Wichita was just like this fellow, hellfire and damnation, but when I happened upon him fucking a man in an alley he ceased such talk. From then on he also took my cock."

As Reed said this, he reached in and pulled out his big cock, which had gotten about halfway hard. He stroked it before me, and I let out a long sigh, as I longed to strip down and have it up me. He pulled on himself and watched me squirm. As the cells were empty since Bob Brown had been dispatched to stand trial at the county seat, he led me to one where he made me strip off my pants.

I sat while Reed put his cock in my mouth and had me suck it until it was wet, after which he had me lie on a cot. "You lie still," he said as he got behind me and pulled my rump up a bit. I felt his prick poke at me, his hands pull me open to reveal my hole. He pushed into me and let out a moan. "Ain't had me a decent fuck since Wichita," he said, "so I'm gonna do you for some time."

His thick cock snaked deep into my bowels, feeling much

like a creature up there, squirming inside me, going deeper and deeper. He set up a rocking motion, like one would on horseback, but he was far short of gallop. Easy canter at first, just in and out, and not seeming to care that someone might come in. The cells were in back, a door separated us from the office, but it was unlocked. I suppose he just didn't give a damn, his need overpowering everything else. That I well understood.

I got a hand under me and took hold of my prick, which was dribbling juice. My balls ached for release. I palmed myself, and the sheriff seemed to like this. "Go to it, boy," he said. "Make yourself squirt while I fuck you."

As he rode me, I pumped my prick, and as I picked up speed so did he. When I unleashed my spunk, I let out a yell and he pushed hard into me, holding me at the waist and driving his big thing deep into my ass. He growled and let go, pounding me, shoving hard and long. I thought about what he was releasing inside me, and I held onto my prick as he did so.

When Reed finished, he pulled out and had me turn over. I looked down: he was still stiff. "Once ain't enough," he told me. I looked at his cock below his gun belt, at the way he'd stayed dressed, had opened only what was needed for the fuck. It made my breath catch, the sight of him like that. I looked up at the shiny silver badge while he reached down and took hold of my spent cock.

He played with me some, pulling on me then feeling my balls. He got me stiff again then leaned down and sucked me into his mouth. I watched as he fed, sucking like a babe on a tit. He didn't touch himself while he did this, and I enjoyed the sight of his big prick standing ready, pointing at me. My ass quivered at the thought of taking it again.

Reed kept at me with his mouth and tongue until I bucked and gave him what he wanted. He sucked and swallowed until

I was dry and even then kept on, as if he needed to suck cock as much as to fuck. Finally he relented.

He went to the basin, washed himself, then soaped his prick. He made me lean against the wall and drove that big piece of meat up me until my hole felt raw. As he fucked me I considered that he probably did it this way most often as men usually coupled quickly, carrying out the act in alleyways and barns and dark streets. Reed was different now, rougher, and I could tell this was a position he favored, that the first had been relief and this was a fuck for enjoyment.

There was no rocking motion now, he was fucking full out, working to get his spunk rising. He growled more than murmured, and he felt like an animal behind me, a big bear or horse with its prick up me. I was hard again but couldn't do anything about it as I needed my hands for support against the wall while he assaulted my bottom. Then he came and roared as he emptied himself, his thrusts rough and hard, as if he were down to the last of his cum and working to get the final drops up out of his balls. When he relented at last and pulled out, I felt weak-kneed and sank onto the cot.

The sheriff looked down at me, both of us breathing hard. I thought about what he'd be like naked, how solid he looked. I wondered if he had a pelt across his chest, one of those thick furs that ran down to the stomach and around the cock. I could see dark hair plentiful at his crotch.

His rod was soft now, and he again went to the basin and washed it, but he didn't button up. He came to me, had me lie back and palm my prick while he put a finger up me. He worked my hole and I worked my rod until I erupted in small spurts. His eyes blazed at the sight. Afterward, he handed me a wet cloth and let me clean myself while he washed again at the basin. Only then did we dress.

"How long you in town?" he asked at the door.

" 'Til my money runs out. Usually don't make last more than a week or two."

"You at the hotel?"

"Room two-twelve."

"I can't be seen going to your room and you can't be here again, not without another scuffle," Reed said. "But I'm riding out tomorrow on business so you can meet me near that old cabin by the stream just east of town. Nine A.M. I'll be in need of you again."

When I left, several curious fellows stopped me. I told them the sheriff had lectured me on the virtues of keeping away from trouble. I didn't linger to hear their response.

It was dusk when I found myself on my own. I went to the livery with the idea of getting my horse and riding to the stream for a twilight swim, but the blacksmith spoke about Clay and I fell to melancholy.

"I know you were friends," Buck said. He was big and burly, his thick bare chest gleaming with sweat. I always thought he'd be a good fuck but knew him to frequent the whores. I said nothing and let him continue. "Found him out back one night, bullet in his head and his pants off, which led to great speculation."

"Does the sheriff suspect anyone?"

"Happened before Reed came on, right after we lost Sheriff Rawlings, so nothing's been done and nobody knows a thing far as I can tell. You might ask Reed to look into it."

I still rode to the stream, stripped, and swam, but I thought of Clay all the while. Because of what Buck had said and because we'd fucked out here in the cover of night. Finally, I lay on the shore and recalled Clay's every inch, fixing not just on his cock but on his face, the smile, his soft curly hair. And I cried a bit.

When I got back to town, the sheriff's office was dark, and I wondered if Reed lay in there naked, prick in hand, thinking maybe of me. It would be a long night for both of us.

The next morning, I didn't attend to my cock as was my habit. I preferred to leave it for the sheriff. I had a good breakfast and rode to the stream where I found his horse tethered. Reed stood on the shore without his coat. I came up behind him, noting again his straightness, as if he bent to no man. His long legs were slightly apart and I saw myself between them, the heavy cock for me to suck.

"Morning," I said as I approached.

He turned and squinted, as the sun was behind me. He nodded but said nothing, his gaze lingering on me as if deciding a thing. Finally he spoke. "I put a blanket down over there," he said, and he indicated where the woods met the shore. He followed me to it. My prick had been hard since before I got off my horse, and when I had undressed for Reed it stood stiff, wet at the tip. He didn't remove a stitch, contented, it seemed, to see me revealed. He drew a long breath, looked me well over, then removed his clothing. Slowly I saw the whole of him, lean but solid and covered in the thick dark hair I'd imagined. It ran the whole front of him, and his erect cock sprang from its nest. Once naked, he handled his thing, his other hand at his balls, which were big and heavy in their bag. As he worked himself he told me to get on the blanket on all fours. When I did, he stood over me. "I'm gonna ride me out a good fuck," he said. "So you just stay still, let me put it up you."

He entered me urgently and pumped in and out as if he hadn't done this for some time. He was a man who could never get enough, who could fuck and fuck and still fuck again. He grunted, pushing his cock in and out, riding me like a horse. I listened to the flow of the stream and the birds who bore witness.

Roaring, the sheriff shoved his prick deep into me, and I felt him release a hot, forceful stream. He rode me hard as he emptied and kept at it for some time, gripping me with powerful hands until the climax passed.

He didn't pull out but remained still. He reached under and took hold of my cock, pulling at it like a cow's teat, milking until I squirted my cream. After I had quieted, he withdrew and led me into the stream where he washed my prick and ass. His big cock grew hard again. He washed himself then led me back to the blanket.

Reed laid me on my side, got his head down at my crotch, and began to suck me. As he slurped he moved around and put his prick to my face and I opened my mouth to it, sucking as much of the shaft as I could. We lay there for some time sucking prick, all else of life far away. I didn't think of Clay or any of the others who had fucked me. I considered only Reed, whose thick cock pushed into my throat, whose dribble I tasted.

After a while I couldn't hold back, and I emptied a frothy load into Reed's mouth. As he swallowed my spunk, I sucked fiercely on his prick, but it delivered nothing. Instead, Reed pulled it out and made me stand. Bending me forward, he put a finger up my hole and felt around inside me. I looked over my shoulder and saw him kneel, pull me open, and get his face down there where no man belonged. I felt his tongue on me. I had to grab my prick as this aroused me no end, the idea of the sheriff licking my hole driving me beyond anything I'd known. Growling in pleasure, he went at me and I bore down to open to him. At that point, he poked in, tongue-fucking me. I unleashed a long moan, and he made agreeable sounds, as if pleased with his meal.

Reed licked for some time, during which I let go a few more squirts. Then he turned me around and licked my rod clean of the drops that remained.

"Lie down," he told me, and I eased onto the blanket. "On your back." He kneeled between my legs then took them and pushed them back so my knees were up around my ears. My hole was exposed, and he looked down at it for some time. "Hold your legs," he commanded, and I did, which freed him to attend to his prick. He worked spit onto it then guided the thing into me. Once inside, he took hold of my legs again, using them for leverage, and he began to drive in and out of me.

As Reed fucked, he looked me over, and I thought he must be one of those who appreciate the whole man, who consider more than just the fuck hole. I had heard of men kissing men but had never experienced such a thing and wondered if the sheriff had done this. I pictured him with his mouth on mine while his prick worked me below. The thought made me clench my hole, at which he issued a rumble of approval.

My prick stiffened yet again as Reed used my bottom. I was as much aroused by the man himself as by the fuck, partly because in my experience men rarely faced each other during the act. It was mostly a cock shoved up an ass and never mind the face, but Reed was looking at me and thereby allowing more. I wondered if he'd done others this way, knowing he probably had, hoping he hadn't.

For some time he thrust in and out of me before he told me he was ready to spend. When he grunted and pushed down harder, I saw his expression change, jaw clenched, face flushed, eyes blazing. I grabbed my pecker and pumped but, being so thoroughly emptied, had nothing left to squirt. Reed seemed pleased with my efforts while he delivered his spunk inside me.

When he finally withdrew he sat back on his haunches, and I noted his big cock finally at rest. Soft now, it hung heavy between his legs, and I longed to hold it in that quiet state but made no move toward him.

"I'd best be getting on with my work," the sheriff said, looking at me as if he wanted no such thing. He lingered a bit more, then stood, went to the stream, and washed himself. I did likewise, and he kept his hands off me. We went to the shore and dressed.

As he rolled the blanket, I told him about Clay. "It happened before you arrived," I said, "and nobody did anything about it. He was stripped and shot, and I don't know who did it, only that my good friend is gone. Could you look into it? Buck, the blacksmith, found the body and may know more than he lets on. I suspect Clay was killed because he fucked men and someone found that intolerable." Reed studied me, and I felt compelled to add, "He fucked me regular."

He nodded, said he would see what he could do, then rode away. I stayed on a bit and walked the shore, as it was a fine day. When I returned to town, I saw nothing of Reed and was careful not to ask after him. I went to the saloon but didn't want to get on with anybody even though one man would have fucked me. That night in my hotel room, I played with my cock for a long time, thinking of Reed fucking me, hoping he was in bed with his big thing stiff for me as well.

I didn't meet up with Reed for three days. He had two men in custody so the cells weren't available, and other times he seemed occupied with work. When I passed him on the street on the night of the third day, he offered me a look that said we would take up again when things permitted. My money had run out, and I would leave town in the morning, so I grew bold and decided to visit the sheriff's office as I had business in the inquiry after Clay's death.

I stopped by late, and he seemed pleased that I did. "I've been tempted to turn men out of the cells so I might have you," he offered. "I want no other."

I looked about the room, ready to do as he pleased, to strip naked then and there should he desire. My cock grew hard, and as I rubbed it, he issued a moan of sorts. "I would take time with you if I could," Reed said, "but we can only go out back for a quick fuck."

This was to my liking, so we went out behind the jail, and I dropped my pants and bent to have him. He grunted throughout, which wasn't long, as he was pent up. He went at me as others had in alleyways, rough and urgent until spurts began. I'd been pulling on my cock and came as well, desiring no more happiness than this.

When Reed had finished he remained in me, prick still hard. He put his arms around me and said once more, "I want no other," which I took to be a statement of his feelings toward me.

"Nor do I," I told him, at which his mouth touched my neck. I knew this was as close to a kiss as he could manage.

We returned to the office where he sat behind his desk and had me sit opposite. "I've learned who may have killed your friend," Reed said, "but there's no proof, so he'll likely remain free."

"Tell me."

"In your absence Clay took up with a man called Charles Robey, a clerk at the general store. He settled here some months ago. Robey's married with children, lives in a house in town, and is churchgoing, respected. Word has it Clay approached him to fuck and was killed as a result, but I don't believe this is so. I suspect Robey is another one who condemns himself for his need of men by lashing out at those very men. We'll never know if he killed Clay, but it's likely he was the one as they were seen talking earlier that night. I've spoken with Robey, who says this was idle conversation. I suspect he killed Clay and probably did it after they had fucked because a man of that sort will always satisfy himself before killing."

I couldn't help crying at this. Reed came to me, put a hand on my shoulder. "You loved the boy," he said.

"I suppose I did."

He went quiet, kept rubbing my shoulder, then spoke softly. "As you heal from your loss maybe one day you'll love again."

I put a hand to his. "One day, yes."

POLE INN

Guy Harris

The sun was just dipping below the mountains as we approached Carson Hole. I was in the back of old Jack's rusty pickup, freezing my butt off, but I didn't care. If I'd known Weaver's foreman was going to be such an asshole I never would have agreed to come work for him in Wyoming. I needed to get away from the ranch to clear my head. I turned and peered through the truck's cab. A tiny cluster of buildings and electric lights glowed up ahead. It looked like something out of *Mad Max*—an outpost of civilization with nothing but vast empty space surrounding it. All around me the swell of the mountains rose up from the edges of the valley before pushing straight into the sky. At least the countryside was pretty here. I pulled my jacket collar higher as the icy air whipped around me.

Seeing as how Carson Hole had the only bar for two hundred miles, folks were charitable enough to call it a town. But it was really just a one-block length of Route 13 with a general store/post office, Riley's Feed and Tools, and the Pole Inn bar. I'd been in the feed store for a few minutes earlier in the week, but this was my first proper visit to town. As we got closer to the lights, I could make out the blue and red neon sign that read POLE INN.

Jack pulled to a stop in the middle of the road, directly across from the bar's sign. There were trucks parked all along the street. Through the closed door of the bar I heard Waylon Jennings on the jukebox and smelled cigarette smoke. Jack rolled down his window, and I hopped out of the side of the truck near his door.

"I'll be drivin' back through 'bout ten o'clock if you need another lift," he said. I nodded my thanks while blowing on my hands and stamping my feet to get warm. He let out a rheumy laugh. "Maybe if they ain't too liquored, you could try and catch yourself a warmer ride with one of them young bucks inside. I expect you'll be plenty cozy in no time, Johnny." He cackled as the truck pulled away. Fever, his white and gray herding dog, gave a loud bark from the passenger seat of the cab.

I stepped onto the sidewalk and brushed off the front of my jacket, then slapped my hands down the length of my jeans to get the dust and hay off. I was bent over with my ass in the air when the door of the bar opened and a woman's voice called out.

"Nice fanny, cowboy."

I stood up quick. She was five foot nothing, but her hair was so tall it just about touched her boyfriend's chin. He was a big man with a brown Stetson and a mean glint in his eye.

"What do you say when a lady gives you a compliment?" he said.

Oh, shit. All I wanted was a damn beer.

Across the street, a man got out of a truck parked in front of Riley's Feed and Tools. He must have been there since before

Jack dropped me off. He sauntered across the street toward us, and my stomach turned over. There was no way I'd be able to fight both him and the guy in the Stetson without getting pummeled. He was tall and muscular, with wide shoulders and long legs. His faded jeans fit like a second skin over well-muscled thighs and lean hips. The sleeves of his plaid shirt were rolled up despite the cold, revealing the kind of thick forearms and broad hands I always associate with men who ride horses for a living.

"Is that what you call a rhetorical question, Cletus?" he said.

Cletus and the girl had turned away from me to face him.

"Stop calling me Cletus, you goat-fucker."

The girl with the big hair put her hand on her boyfriend's arm as if to hold him back, but all the earlier threat had gone out of his voice.

"Now, Cletus," the newcomer drawled, "you know as well as anyone that goats aren't my thing."

Cletus froze for a second then abruptly stalked off down the street, his girlfriend half-running to keep up. He got into a Dodge Ram with oversize wheels, paying no mind to the girl, who stood on the sidewalk by the passenger door, tapping her foot.

"I'm betting fifteen seconds," the stranger said. He started counting them off. At fourteen, the girl jerked the door open herself and got into the truck. He laughed. "I was close. He should know better than to get Rhonda mad."

He turned toward me, and I looked directly at his face for the first time. He was still grinning, full lips revealing even white teeth. His eyes were friendly and mischievous at the same time. My cock hardened in my jeans as he smiled at me. I was glad I'd worn my shirt untucked.

I held out my hand. "I'm Johnny."

He shook my hand, and a surge of heat went straight to my crotch. "Hank," he said. "Why don't you let me buy you a drink to make up for Cletus's bad manners?" He opened the door to the bar. I thought I felt his hand on my back through my jacket as we walked in, but I couldn't be sure.

Inside, people filled all the booths and tables, and it was standing room only at the long wooden bar on the right. A pair of ski poles crisscrossed the mirror behind the bar, framing a broad-shouldered, beefy bartender whipping out drinks with graceful speed.

"I didn't think there were this many people in all of Wyoming," I said.

Hank laughed and cut through the crowd at the bar. "Beer okay?" he asked.

"Yep."

He held up two fingers to the bartender, who nodded and continued setting drinks on a tray for a waitress in skintight jeans. A few minutes later the bartender came over and set two draft beers in front of us. "You must be the new hand up at Weaver's place," he said. I nodded.

"Johnny, meet Owen Rideout," Hank said. "Best bartender in Carson Hole, and not a bad horseman either."

Owen winked at me. "I'm the *only* bartender in Carson Hole, but I'll take any compliment I can get." He was probably forty or so, and handsome in a rugged way. The sheer size of his muscles made him imposing, but the laugh lines around his eyes and mouth matched his easygoing manner. I imagined he didn't have much trouble keeping peace in the bar.

Hank pulled out some cash, but Owen waved it away. "On me. Nice to meet you, Johnny. I hope we can say hello properly when things slow down a bit." He nodded at Hank with a twinkle in his eye then moved off down the bar.

His hand on my elbow, Hank guided me toward the back of the room. When we first came in, I hadn't noticed the narrow door at the far end of the bar, but as we drew closer I heard the sound of pool balls clicking off each other.

"Want to play a game? It's quieter back there," Hank said.

I wanted to do anything that let me look at him a little longer. I nodded yes. There were five pool tables and four dartboards in the back room, along with a glass door that seemed to lead to an outdoor deck. All the pool tables were in use, so Hank and I played a few games of darts. The waitress came through every once in a while to deliver more drinks. We tipped her, but she refused money for the beers. "Owen says it's all on the house for you boys tonight."

Between throws at the dartboard, Hank told me about himself and his cattle ranch, which was about thirty miles down Route 13, nestled up against the mountains. "You wouldn't believe what the Japanese will pay for good Angus beef," he said.

"I expect you're right."

"What about you?" he asked. "What brought you out to Weaver's place?"

"Running cattle," I told him.

"You have family in Wyoming?"

"California."

"California, huh? That's nice."

I nodded.

"Do you miss it?"

"Sometimes."

"Do you like Wyoming?"

"Yes and no."

"You're not much of a talker, are you?" he said with a smile.

I shook my head.

He threw back his head and laughed. "All right, Johnny, let's play a new game."

A table had opened up, and Hank took two pool cues off the wall and handed one to me. I tried not to stare as he leaned over the table to rack the balls. His wide shoulders tapered down to narrow hips and a perfectly rounded ass. He picked up two blocks of chalk and suddenly turned to toss one to me. I wasn't sure if he'd seen me staring at him. His eyes lingered on mine as he slowly rubbed the chalk over the tip of his cue. When he leaned over the table again to line up the cue ball I thought I might come in my jeans.

He turned back to me, casually running his hand down his cue. I wished I was that stick. If my cock got any harder I'd have to go jack off in one of the bathroom stalls, drunk cowboys right outside taking leaks. I thanked god again for my untucked shirt.

"Why don't you take the first shot?" he said.

We played two games before I relaxed enough to hit the balls somewhat regularly. Hank went out of his way to put me at ease, asking me questions and not seeming to mind my short answers. As we continued playing, the room started to clear out. The waitress came in and announced last call.

As we played, I found myself transfixed by Hank's hands, imagining how they'd feel on my ass, my dick. Several times I thought I caught him staring at me. The rhythm of the game, the way he moved around the table—I was mesmerized.

The waitress popped her head in again and said, "Owen told me to ask if you're sure you don't want anything else." Suddenly I realized the back room was empty except for us.

Hank looked at me and I shook my head no. "I think we're all set, Dotty," he said. "Thanks for taking such good care of us tonight." He tried to hand her some bills, but she waved them away.

"You've tipped me enough already tonight, Hank. And Owen says I get to cut out early 'cause ya'll are the last ones here."

When she had gone, Hank looked around at the empty room then grinned at me. "How about a wager?"

"What kind?" I said.

"If I miss this shot, you can dare me to do anything you want."

"And if you don't miss?"

"Then I can dare you," he said.

I licked my lips, and his eyes flicked to my mouth and stayed there.

"Deal," I said.

He gave me a wicked smile, and I felt a quiver all the way from my cock to my ass.

Hank surveyed the table for a while, making a show that this was serious business. He pointed to a ball with his cue and then to a side pocket. He lined up the shot and took two tentative strokes before thrusting the cue forward. The balls smacked together then slid smoothly across the felt, the ball dropping gently into the pocket.

"Looks like I made it," Hank said. He stood there looking at me until heat coursed through my body.

"Looks that way," I said.

Hank came over and took the cue out of my hand. For a second he stayed there, inches in front of me. I smelled the soap on his skin, noticed the five o'clock shadow along his jaw. A vein pulsed in his muscular neck, making me think of his cock and what it would be like to run my tongue over his skin. Then he laid both our sticks on the pool table. "Let me show you something," he said.

He walked ahead of me toward the glass door at the back of the room and I stared greedily at his beautiful ass and thighs. Then I noticed his reflection in the glass. He was watching me

watching him, lust and amusement mingled in his expression. I
held his gaze and smiled.

Hank opened the door. "After you," he said. As I walked
past him, I let my hand brush against his crotch. He let out a
small gasp, and I could feel his hardness through his jeans.

We were on a deck insulated on all sides by glass. The dark
emptiness of the valley slid away for miles toward the uprising
of the mountains, and the sky was bright with stars. It was cold
out here compared to the bar, but not like it'd been in the back
of Jack's pickup. It suddenly occurred to me that I'd long since
missed my ride back to the ranch. But I didn't care. Hank came
and stood next to me facing the view, his leg touching mine. I
reached over and dragged my hand slowly up the top of his thigh,
stopping right next to his crotch. He turned so his body faced
mine, and I traced my fingers along his inner thigh. I heard his
breath catch as I stopped again just before reaching his cock.

"You like to tease, don't you?" he whispered. I grinned at
him in the half dark, and he licked his lips.

"I'm going to make you moan," he said with a wicked smile.
My cock pulsed.

There were chairs and tables all over the deck, but he guided
me backward until I was leaning against the back wall of the
building. He ran his hands up my thighs then cupped my ass.
"I've been wanting to do that since I saw you get out of that
pickup," he said.

I unbuttoned his shirt, pulling it off him and stroking his
muscular arms. "And I've been wanting to do this." I kissed
the pulse in his neck, tasting the salt on his skin. Then I ran my
lips over the springy hair on his chest and forearms. I lifted his
right hand and sucked a finger into my mouth, surprised by the
smoothness of his skin. His lips parted as he watched me, then
he pulled off my jacket and unbuttoned my shirt.

"Is Owen likely to come back here and find us?" I asked.

"It'll take him a good hour or more to close up."

He got my shirt off me and ran his hands over my biceps and chest. "Looking good, Johnny." He let his fingers trail down my abdomen. A shiver coursed through me, but he stopped short of my cock.

"Turnabout is fair play," he whispered devilishly. He explored my mouth with his lips and tongue while running his hands over my stomach again. I reached for his pants, but he held both my wrists together with one of his hands and pulled them over my head. He kissed my neck, stroking me everywhere but my cock with his free hand. I arched against him, but he pushed me back against the wall. He ran his tongue lightly against my lower lip, unbuttoning the top button of my jeans and slowly pulling down the zipper.

"What do you want, Johnny?" he said. Still holding both my wrists together, he kissed me deeper. He edged my jeans and underwear down below my hips and ran his hand over my naked thighs and ass. My cock was standing straight up, aching for release. I moaned.

"That's what I wanted to hear," he said. He gave me his wicked grin, then brought his free hand up and licked the length of it. When he finally touched my cock, I thought I would explode. He seemed to know exactly how far he could push things before pulling back. After bringing me to the edge several times, he said again, "What do you want, Johnny?" My cock throbbed in his warm hand as he stroked and stroked me.

All I could do was groan. He rubbed me faster, sliding his knee gently between my legs until it rested against my balls with steady pressure. I clenched my thighs around him. I wanted to touch him, but he held my wrists firmly against the wall above my head.

"Oh, god," I moaned into his mouth. Hot spurts shot over my stomach and chest. "Oh, god. Oh, god."

He looked down to admire his handiwork, then brought his mouth back to mine, letting go of my hands. They tingled as I brought them down and the blood flowed back into them. He pulled a bandana out of his back pocket and helped me wipe myself off.

"Now you," I said, reaching for him. I could see his hard-on through his jeans.

"I think we'd better check on Owen first."

I looked at his crotch.

He grinned as he buttoned up his shirt. "Oh, don't worry about that. You still owe me a dare, remember?"

I finished putting my clothes back on, and he led the way back into the bar. My legs felt unsteady.

The jukebox had been turned down, but Patsy Cline's voice filled every corner of the dimly lit room. Owen, shirtless now, stacked crates of empties. The neon beer signs above the bar reflected colors off the sheen of sweat on his torso—huge, thickly muscled shoulders, massive biceps, and a slightly round, taut belly. He squatted to lift another case, and I stared at the bulge of his thick thighs, straining his jeans. If I hadn't come just minutes before, my cock would have been at full attention.

I excused myself to go to the men's room while Hank continued over to Owen. Just before I went into the bathroom I heard Hank say, "You're such a show-off." Owen laughed.

In the bathroom, I took a leak and cleaned myself up. When I opened the men's room door I saw Hank sitting on a barstool, Owen across from him polishing the bar with a towel.

"...closeted hick," Owen said.

"That's Cletus for you. But how can I blame him for hating

me? It must be depressing knowing your first lay is the best you'll ever have."

Owen flicked Hank with the towel. "I've always loved your modesty best."

"What a lie," Hank said. "You always said it was my sweet ass."

Owen looked up and saw me. "Hey there, Johnny."

I smiled at him.

"I hear you had a cold ride into town. That Jack treats his dog better than the Queen of England."

I took a seat next to Hank while Owen rubbed the towel over the bar in front of me. I couldn't help staring at the play of muscles in his arms and chest as he stroked the wood. The hair on his chest was dark and springy, tapering down invitingly to the top of his jeans. He saw me watching him and smiled. In the mirror behind the bar I saw Hank roll his eyes indulgently.

"I can make coffee if you'd like something hot," Owen said.

"Thanks," I said, "but I'm pretty warm already." I put my hand on Hank's thigh and ran my fingers toward his crotch.

"Are you up to your old tricks again?" Hank said.

I grinned and shrugged.

"Johnny likes to tease," he said.

"Not as much as you do," I replied. I looked at Owen, who was glancing between my hand and face to see what I'd do next. He'd stopped wiping down the bar, and was clenching the towel in one hand. I smiled at him then let my eyes travel back down his happy trail. The bulge in his pants looked as big as the rest of him. I turned to look at Hank, who was giving me his wicked grin.

"You don't even need to be dared, do you Johnny?" Hank said.

"Don't stand on ceremony on my account," Owen said.

That was all the encouragement I needed. I rubbed my hand over Hank's hard-on, then unbuttoned his fly. His cock sprang out, reaching toward the ceiling. It was long and thick, the head glistening with creamy precum. All I could think of was getting it into my mouth. But his wasn't the only cock I was hoping to suck that night. I looked over at Owen, whose hard nipples and shallow breathing told me he was more than ready to get in the game. Hank seemed to read the indecision in my eyes about where to start first, and laughed out loud.

"Don't worry, Johnny. You'll have as many chances as you want at this rodeo."

"Seeing as how we all just met," Owen said, "we ought to tell you both Hank and I are clean. But I've got plenty of skins if you'd feel more comfortable."

A cowboy *and* a gentleman, I thought. It was good to meet such nice people after being treated like crap all week at the ranch.

"Same for me," I said. "And I want you to know just how much I appreciate your hospitality." Without another pause I slid off my barstool and took Hank's cock into my mouth. Owen laughed, and Hank laugh-moaned as I circled the head of his cock with my tongue. A minute later I heard Owen vault up onto the bar for a closer view. Without taking my mouth off Hank's cock, I used both my hands to pull his pants down farther. I sensed him taking off his shirt, but all my focus was on the feel of his cock in my mouth. When I'd freed his thighs and ass, I used my right hand to hold him in position so I could take him further into my mouth. I sucked down as much as I could, coming back again and again to the sweet spot on the underside of his shaft with my tongue. I cupped his balls with my left hand, feeling them tighten and pull up as I worshipped every inch of his sweet cock.

The sound of Hank's moans and the thought of Owen watching got me so hot that my own cock battled to escape my jeans. I turned my head a bit so I could check out what Owen was up to on the bar and it nearly made me come in my pants. He had taken off his jeans and boots and was sitting on the edge of the bar buck naked with his legs on either side of Hank. His massive cock was inches from Hank's face, and Hank was taking full advantage by licking it like an ice cream cone. The sight of Hank's gorgeous mouth all over that enormous cock made me tingle from my dick to my asshole. I renewed my attention to Hank, imagining that as I sucked his cock, I was somehow also sucking Owen's. I was moaning now too, and that sent Hank over the edge. His cock pulsed in my mouth as the first spurt of jizz hit the back of my throat. I kept licking and sucking, more gently now as the spurts kept coming. When he was done, I had a mouth full of cum and a smile the size of Texas.

I looked up to see Hank still sucking Owen off. He was using one hand to keep Owen's dick in place, the other to tease his ass. Owen looked at me, his face ecstatic at witnessing two blow jobs at once, one of them performed on him. I had an idea for Hank's cum, which was still in my mouth, but I paused to admire the contrast between Owen's meaty build and Hank's lean, sinewy body. Hank was sweaty and flushed with orgasm, and Owen's hands clenched the bar, making the muscles in his forearms and biceps bulge. I couldn't believe I had not one but two gorgeous men naked in front of me.

I ran a hand up Owen's thick thigh and moved in to join Hank on his cock. Owen groaned when he felt the second mouth on his dick. I let Hank's cum dribble out all over the shaft, giving Hank and me extra lubrication as we slid our tongues and lips all over Owen's massive girth. Our mouths met at the head, a three-way French kiss with Owen's cock in the middle.

Having seen the way Owen responded to Hank's ass-teasing, I used one of my hands to massage some of Hank's jizz over Owen's balls and asshole. Owen squirmed toward my fingers, so I inserted one and was rewarded by an instant surge in his cock. I gently stroked in and out while my tongue lapped up and down his shaft and Hank worked the tip. Owen let out a huge groan and his ass tightened around my finger. I kept licking his shaft as Hank caught the cum load in his mouth. My own dick was so hard now that my precum was sticky in my jeans.

Hank seemed aware of my situation, and while Owen recovered, he motioned for me to strip and get up on the bar. I released my aching cock first, then took off my shirt and jacket. Hank and Owen watched appreciatively. I hopped up next to Owen but Hank shook his head and gestured for me to lie down on my back. When I was spread out naked on the bar he got up next to me and knelt between my thighs. He took my throbbing cock in his mouth and let Owen's hot cum drip all over me, rubbing it all the way down to my balls and asshole.

"Like I said, Johnny, turnabout is fair play." He grinned up at me from between my thighs, Owen's cum glistening on his full lips. I thought I was going to shoot my load right then, but I managed to hang on. Hank gestured to the mirror behind the bar and said, "I thought you might like the view." Owen took the hint. As he moved the bottles away from the base of the mirror, the muscles in his back rippled and his firm asscheeks flexed. In the mirror I saw Hank's sleek body kneeling over mine, his head bobbing over my cock. I nearly came right then, but Hank sensed it and pulled back. He toyed with me, lightly licking the underside of my shaft and running his fingers gently over my balls and asshole. When Owen was done adjusting the bottles, he came around to the customer side of the bar and stood next to my head.

"How you doing, Johnny?" he said.

Hank took that as his cue to begin working my cock more thoroughly, licking, sucking, and deep-throating while increasing his ass-teasing as well.

My response to Owen came out as an unintelligible moan. He laughed and kissed me, immediately working his way over my neck and chest as Hank kept sucking me and fondling my ass. I turned again to the mirror to watch but had to look away. My whole body was so ripe to come that I was tingling all over. And I didn't want it to end.

Hank worked my ass in earnest now. Owen's jizz was the perfect lubricant, and I was greedy for more. I was so out of my mind that at that moment I thought I could take even Owen's fat cock in my ass and love every inch of it. But that would have meant stopping what was happening, and there was no way I was doing that. Hank slipped another finger into me as Owen worked his way down my stomach with licks and kisses. Panting and moaning, I spread my legs wider as Owen's head nudged into my crotch.

I didn't want to come yet, but I had to watch. I looked down at the tops of their heads moving on me, their sweet asses in the air. Then I looked at the mirror and saw Owen's face framed below Hank's, his big pink tongue headed for my balls. Hank was gulping a throatful of cock, his arm flexing as he pumped his fingers in my ass. The sight burned itself into my brain and went straight to my cock. Just as Owen's fat tongue lapped my nuts, I came like a fucking rocket. I shuddered and bucked, riding Hank's fingers in my ass, both of their mouths all over me. Owen kept licking my balls, but Hank moved his mouth off me so he could watch my cum load shoot up over all of us and onto the bar. He grinned at me as I writhed and moaned.

When I was done, Owen surfaced, and both he and Hank

moved up the bar to lie down on either side of me. The three of us lay on our backs laughing as I caught my breath.

"Welcome to Carson Hole, Johnny," Hank said.

"We hope you can stay awhile," Owen said.

"He has to stay," Hank said. "He still owes me a dare."

LONGHORNS

Victor J. Banis

They were roping cattle when he showed up. "Heard you was herding some longhorns," he said. "Thought you could use an extra hand. Name's Buck."

Les looked him over. The stranger wore an old shirt, faded but clean, and those new pants—dungarees, the boys called them—they said were more comfortable than old-fashioned woolies. He wasn't more than eighteen, maybe nineteen, and small built but wiry, his skin leather colored. His hair was a mass of curls, black as obsidian; his eyes, in the fading light, nearly as dark.

"You Indian?" Les asked.

"Half." He seemed unembarrassed by the fact. "Daddy was a trader, so's I heard. Mama was a Nasoni."

"Don't know that tribe."

"Texas is a Nasoni word. Means *friend*. I'm a friendly sort." Buck grinned again and surveyed Les up and down. Something about the way he looked at him made Les uncomfortable.

"You new around here? I don't recall seeing you."

"Just come up from Galveston."

Les looked past him to where the boys were working on the corral. "Best make that a little higher, Red," he called. "Looks like we might get some weather."

When he turned his gaze back, the kid was looking down. Les looked too, and realized Buck was staring right at the bulge of his crotch.

"What you got on your mind?" he said sharply.

"I was just thinking…" Buck seemed not to mind at all that he'd been caught staring. "…'Bout some of the things them sailors taught me down in Galveston."

"Well, they ain't no sailors here," Les said, doubly annoyed because he'd been out on the prairie weeks now, and his prick, on alert for any prospects, took note of the attention. "I reckon you can stick around for a day or two, see how it goes. I guess you can ride," he added spitefully. "We ain't got room for sissies."

"Well, now, seeing it's you, I'd surely love the opportunity to show just how well I can ride," Buck said with a flash of teeth in his sun-leathered face. "I got the time, if you got the inclination."

"I expect I'll see you on your horse soon enough," Les said.

"Oh, a horse, well, I guess so." Buck turned and started away, but he looked back over his shoulder to add, "I can ride them, too, case that's what you meant."

Watching him go, Les wondered if he had just made himself a mistake.

The Texas longhorn was the descendant of the cattle the Spanish explorers had brought. Narrow-hipped, swaybacked, bony, the longhorn adapted to the wilderness with a vengeance. They could fight off wolves and wildcats, even a bear. They ignored

LONGHORNS 149

blizzard and drought and could travel forever. They lived mostly in a no-man's-land of mesquite, prickly pear cactus and sharp-thorned paloverde, rattlesnake, and javelina. No man pretended it was easy to catch the longhorn. On the other hand, any man who could, owned them, and they were the animal for the long, arduous cattle drives to the railroads in Kansas.

Les and his men had herded better than a thousand head by now and would shortly bring them to the ranch to prepare for the drive up the Chisholm. The weather was hot, and the cow-hands worked with sweat streaming down their faces and kept an eye on the sky. So far, they'd had no trouble, and they were all looking forward to heading home. Les figured even if the new man was a mite strange, he couldn't likely cause too much mischief in the few days they had left.

Les was sleeping lightly that night in the weighted heat, when someone shouted his name. Just as he opened his eyes, a sheet of lightning lit up the prairie sky. He scrambled up, instantly awake. A bad thunderstorm could stampede the cattle. The temporary corral wouldn't withstand the onslaught of a thousand or more charging longhorns.

Distant thunder rumbled ominously. In the next flash, he saw the men hastily saddling horses. They all knew what had to be done. If the cattle stampeded, the only necessity was to stop them. How, you couldn't be sure until you'd done it, or failed.

The cattle were on their feet, too, milling nervously. The cowboys riding guard began to sing to calm them. *"Did you ever hear of Sweet Betsy from Pike...."*

In another flash of light, Les saw a rider wearing one of those new rubberized slickers. The light was gone too quickly for him to see who was wearing it. In the next moment, he forgot cow-boy and slicker. The cowhands were singing louder and louder, the air dense, heavier, the movement of the cattle more worried.

An ear-splitting clap of thunder rent the air, and a blinding blue flash set the night sky afire. In the blackness that followed, Les was blinded, but he didn't have to see to know what was making the earth tremble. The cattle were stampeding. The storm had unleashed torrents of rain, but it was the thunder and lightning that spooked the cattle and each rider cursed as he rode in pursuit of the thundering, bellowing herd.

Les rode for all he was worth, his palomino nearly leaping from under him. You had to get to the front of the herd to turn a stampede. Once, twice, lightning flashed, and he saw not only the herd but the rain-slickered cowboy just off to his right, riding alongside him, hell bent for leather.

The ground shook beneath pounding hooves. Despite the rain, he felt the heat of a thousand rangy bodies. The smell of cowhide filled his wet nostrils, and the palomino snorted wildly. Les could see nothing ahead or below. One misstep—a prairie dog hole, a fallen branch—and both horse and rider would end up with broken necks. The banging of horns was like the clicking of castanets in a Mexican fandango, but this was a deadly dance, and the thunder-drums and the alto cries of the cattle only made it eerier.

The sky turned blue-white again, and glancing aside, Les saw that they were alongside the leaders of the herd, him and Red, and somehow the rain-slickered rider had gotten ahead of them, pounding stride for stride in a life-or-death race with the front-running bull. To turn the cattle from their headlong flight, they had to push them aside, and that meant the rain-slickered rider had to convince the leader. If that cowboy fell, if his horse stumbled for an instant, those charging hooves would pound them into the Texas dust.

They were turning. The lead bull yielded, veered, and once

the leaders had started, the others followed, slowly forming a circle that wound in upon itself, until cattle bumped into cattle and none of them knew which way to run.

The stampede was stopped. The thunder grew more distant, the lightning far-off flashes. Les and the palomino were both gasping for air. He leaned down and patted the horse's powerful neck, and it snorted disdainfully.

Till morning, the boys would take turns riding a containing circle about the gradually calming cattle. With daylight the cattle would be penned again, corral repaired, damage assessed.

Les felt oddly exhilarated as he rode back to camp. Cookie's campfire already glimmered where he brewed thick bitter coffee by the gallon in his big enameled pot, to keep the men awake.

The cowboys milled about, laughing off their fear, slapping each other's backs. Les dismounted next to the campfire. Red saw him and called, "Man, did you see that kid ride? I never seen nothing like that!"

"The one in the slicker? I saw him," Les said. "But who...?"

He didn't need to finish, because the new man rode up just then and jumped down from his horse, shed the slicker, and tossed it across his saddle.

"Hoo-ee," he shouted, walking over to them. "That was some excitement, wasn't it? Got my blood all stirred up." He reached behind him and rubbed his hands over his butt. "Makes me want a ridin' myself, to take the edge off." He cast an unmistakable glance at Les's crotch. To Les's embarrassment, the boys standing nearby saw it too and whooped with laughter, too keyed up themselves to mind.

"Say," Red said with a wide grin on his face, clapping a hand on Buck's shoulder, "why don't you and me go take care of them horses?"

Buck returned his grin and started away with him, but he

looked back to wink at Les, which produced another round of
guffaws. One or two of the cowboys looked after the departing
pair wistfully.

Les was no fool. Sometimes on the trail, he knew, one or the
other of the men would slip away to somebody else's bedroll for
a spell. Everyone pretended they didn't notice or hear the noises;
it might be *you* feeling the need the next night. Truth was, once
or twice he kind of wished someone might creep over to his bedroll, but they never had.

He suddenly realized his eyes had strayed to Buck's curvy
little bottom, those tight dungarees like a second skin. He had
a fleeting notion he wouldn't have minded taking the edge off
his own pent-up energy. He turned away in disgust. *Shit,* he told
himself. *Next thing you know I'll be taking him serious.*

Fucker sure could ride, though.

What surprised Les over the next few days even more than
Buck's outrageous remarks and leers was that none of the
grizzled cowboys seemed to take any offense. Course, Buck had
proven himself the night of the stampede. These were tough
hombres—a man with that kind of nerve, who could ride like
that, could talk and act however he wanted, was their attitude.
If anything, they seemed to take an amused interest in his bla-
tant flirtation with their range boss.

Well, way things were, Les couldn't fire their hero now.
He'd have an uprising on his hands, so Buck came back with
them to the Double H. Anyway, Les figured, all them boys in
the bunkhouse, Buck'd probably find somebody who'd be happy to give him those rides he craved, and the newcomer would
be out of Les's hair.

It didn't work out that way. He should have guessed
something when he sat down to breakfast two days later

and discovered Cookie's skills had miraculously improved.

"These flapjacks are light as feathers," Les said. "What'd you do to make them different, Cookie?"

"Weren't me," Cookie said. "It's that new boy. He's natural-born cook."

Les almost choked on a swallow of coffee—better coffee, too, than the usual brew. "He's cooking now?"

"Sure is. Been teaching me all kinds of things. You'd be surprised."

"Maybe I wouldn't," Les said.

"I even told him he could have my little room behind the kitchen there, to sleep in," Cookie said on his way out. "And I'd take me the shed."

When Les asked Buck about it, why he wasn't sleeping with the others at the bunkhouse, he said, "I figured you wasn't likely to stroll down to the bunkhouse at night, but, hell, you could sleepwalk your way here."

"I ain't one for sleepwalking," Les said, and started to turn away, but he paused to ask, "Didn't you ever have no women, boy?"

"Some."

"You didn't like it?"

Buck shrugged. "Well, sure, who doesn't? You think I'm queer or somethin'?"

"I think you're something, that's for sure. So how's come if you like women, you're always trying to get someone to, you know?"

"Well, see, when I was in Galveston, this lady, Miz Montgomery, ran a boarding house, and every Sunday she fixed fried chicken, and that was some delicious chicken. I never could get my fill, but the thing is, much as I loved that chicken, it never stopped me enjoying a big old juicy steak. 'Sides, if you want to know, I can do things with a piece of beef that old lady couldn't ever do with her hens."

"Seems to me the steer might have some say in that," Les said. "We got work to do, boy." He walked away, but he knew without looking that Buck was staring at his ass, and it made him self-conscious.

He found Buck a few days later, looking over a pony that was penned up by itself.

"Don't be looking at that horse, boy," he said, "Ain't no one on this ranch been able to ride him. I'm just keeping him to breed."

"That's an Indian horse," Buck said, as if that explained everything.

"What that horse is is the devil himself."

"Here, let me show you." Buck jumped over the fence, and Les came up to the rail.

"That pony liked to kill old Jack when he got too close," he warned.

" 'Cause he was afraid," Buck said. "They smell fear."

There was nothing for Les to do but jump over the fence after him. Some of the boys saw the two of them in the corral and drifted over to see what was happening.

The pinto watched them approach and danced about skittishly, but it kept his eyes on Buck and seemed to be waiting for him. Buck came up to him without pause, and taking hold of his head, he said, "You gotta breathe into its nostrils, like so." He snorted hard and loud up the horse's nostrils. To Les's surprise, the horse responded in kind, its nostrils flaring as it breathed a powerful stream of air into the Nasoni's face.

"It's the horse's way of greeting a friend," Buck said. "Now you do it."

Les approached, feeling a little foolish. The pinto whinnied, but its large limpid eyes regarded him with a steady appraisal and it remained motionless. Les leaned forward till his nose almost touched the pinto's, and breathed out hard, up the animal's nostrils. He was rewarded with a blast of hot breath that all but choked him.

"Again," Buck said. Les repeated the ritual. "Now," he said, "he's your friend. You can ride him anywhere."

By now the men were crowded along the fence, staring, no one making a sound. The horse snorted, as if wondering what all the fuss was about. When Les reached up to pet its muzzle, the horse rubbed gently against his hand.

"Well, I'll be a son of a bitch," Les said. "You really think he'd let me get on?"

"Won't neither one of us try to throw you if you want a ride," Buck said.

The men at the fence laughed loudly. Les blushed crimson, but when Buck put out his hands for a stirrup, he stepped into them and swung a long leg over the pony's back. There was a moment of silence, everyone holding his breath. Les took hold of the pony's mane, and a minute later the cowboys saw their boss riding the devil horse bareback around the corral.

That night, Les finished his chores and came out of the barn to find some of the boys throwing knives at a crudely drawn bull's-eye they'd tacked to a fence post. As he watched, Buck took a throw and hit the target dead center.

Jack saw Les and nodded in his direction. "Now there's the champeen knife thrower in these parts," he said.

"That right?" Buck gave him a speculative look. "How's about a little friendly competition. Take turns. First one misses the target loses."

"Ain't much of a target," Les said.

"I got a better one for you, if you're interested," Buck told him, and the men chuckled.

"Somebody give me a knife," Les said. He took Jack's, stepped to the line scratched in the dust, and threw. The knife hit the target just off the bull's-eye.

Buck took a turn. His Bowie struck dead center again.

Les's next throw was dead center too, then Buck tossed one that just caught the edge of the target. Les threw another bull's-eye, but Buck's next throw missed the target and thudded into the wood of the fence post.

Les handed Jack back his knife and started away without a word. Buck came after him. "Let's make it three out of five," he said.

Les stopped dead still. "Your trouble," he said, "is you just can't stand the idea of me topping you."

"Well, now, ain't that exactly what I've been talking about for days: you topping me?" Buck said.

"Shit fire," Les snapped and stomped away. What really riled him was that he had been thinking, just now looking at him, that the damned half-breed reminded him of a puppy, all rambunctious and jumping around and wagging his tail. Kind of cute, in a way.

Keep thinking that way, he warned himself, *next thing you'll be plugging that hot butt for him.* And that was never going to happen.

His dick took the idea seriously, though.

On Saturday nights the hands generally rode into San Antone to let off a little steam. Les was surprised to find, when they had all left the following Saturday, Buck was still there.

"I thought maybe if it was just the two of us here," Buck

said, grinning. "Nobody would know, is what I mean."

"Afraid it's going to be just the one of you. I got to go into town too, but I'm taking the buckboard so I can load up on supplies." He thought for a minute. "Tell you what, why don't you come along and we'll make a stop at Miz Yolanda's. That is, if you can handle a woman."

"Sounds like fun," Buck agreed enthusiastically.

Trouble was, it wasn't, not for Les, though it surely sounded like it was for Buck. He was in the next cubicle. The arrangements at Yolanda's didn't allow much privacy. Buck had ended up picking not one but two girls—one didn't look much more than a kid herself, and the other was a big one with a hearty laugh and enormous tits. He could hear the three of them in there, laughing and chatting, and then the bedsprings commenced to creak, faster and louder. All kinds of moaning and groaning ensued, then some more fooling, before the bed started up again. Christ, didn't he ever get tired?

Les wasn't doing so well, though. He had chosen Rosita, who he'd had before, but he couldn't seem to get going. He tried a couple times, without success, and blamed that damned racket next door. He worked on himself a bit and tried again while he kept his ear cocked to the wall. Finally, he gave up and put his trousers back on. He'd already paid Yolanda, but he took a dollar out of his pocket and tossed the coin to the girl.

"I guess we don't have to tell anybody about this," he said.

"I won't tell, señor. I promise," Rosita said, smiling.

He figured by tomorrow everybody at Yolanda's would know.

Except for Buck's tuneless whistling, the two men were silent in the buckboard on the way home. Not until they had reached the open country did Buck ask, "How'd you do with little Rosita?"

"Just fine," Les said in a hearty voice, while his pecker called him a liar. "I pleasured her twice." He paused. "You took care of both those gals?"

"Hell, I could've took two more."

"You bragging?"

Buck laughed. "No, I swear, no matter how much I pump it, that well never runs dry." The silence descended again. Les was aware of Buck looking sideways at him. He hoped his hard-on didn't show. Damned thing had developed a mind of its own lately.

"You still randy?" Buck asked.

"Nope." Les swallowed hard. "Not after that workout Rosita gave me."

"Well, *he* don't look tired." Buck reached across and gave Les's erection a friendly squeeze.

Les was so surprised he couldn't think straight. His impulse was to shove Buck's hand away, but somehow his hands wouldn't do it, and his dick was threatening to burst some buttons. He tried to say something, and opened his mouth, but all that came out was a kind of sputter.

Buck fumbled with the fly. Of its own accord, Les's butt scooted forward a little to make the buttons easier, and a minute later his dick jumped free.

"Jesus," Buck said. "That is a pecker and a half."

Despite himself, Les felt a flush of pride. He swallowed again. He'd never had nobody else's hand stroke his cock. He'd figured it would feel the same as his own hand, but it felt different. Felt good, actually. That kind of worried him.

That wasn't but the beginning, though. To Les's astonishment, Buck leaned across the seat, lowered his head, and put his mouth on Les's dick. Les near jumped out of his seat. "You oughtn't do that," he said. "What if someone was to see?"

"Out here?" Buck laughed. "Ain't nobody out here but that coyote over yonder. Who's he gonna tell?"

Buck took it in his mouth again. Les wanted to object but couldn't. He'd heard about blow jobs and always wondered, but he'd never gotten up the courage to ask Yolanda's girls to do it, afraid they'd think he was queer. Now, here he was with Buck slobbering all over his knob with that hot, wet mouth, the tongue flicking around under the flange. He gasped as Buck took all ten inches down his throat.

Between unfinished business at Yolanda's, and what Buck was doing, Les came all too quickly. His entire body seemed to be erupting out of his cockhead into that hungry mouth.

"Hoo-ee!" Buck said, licking his lips. "You had all that left after Rosita?"

"I got me a pretty good well, too," Les said dryly.

"We got miles yet to go," Buck said, and would have resumed sucking, but Les put his hand down and pushed him away.

"I'm fine," he said. He tucked his dick back into his trousers, not without some difficulty—it was still half hard and didn't want to go.

Buck shrugged and sat up on his side of the seat. They rode the rest of the way in silence.

Les stopped the buckboard by the kitchen door. "I'll say good night," he said.

"I'll help you with the supplies," Buck said.

"No need. I'll unload everything myself."

"Hell, I'll gladly help you with a load anytime."

"Listen...," Les said. He had been thinking the rest of the trip about what to say. "What happened back there, hell, I was curious, that's all. I never had nobody do that before, but don't you be getting ideas. I ain't queer neither."

"A man likes what he likes."

"You can like all you like," Les said. "Just don't expect it to happen again. I was just curious."

Buck jumped to the ground and grinned up at him. "Well, you get curious again, you know where I sleep," he said. "Maybe I'll grease my butthole, just in case."

Even in the moonlight, Les's blush was obvious. "You have a good night's sleep," he said, and drove toward the barn.

It was a good hour before Les got everything put away and the horses settled. He came through the kitchen and, seeing a faint glow of light from Buck's room, he went and looked in. Buck was naked on his pallet, back to the door. His round little butt looked as soft and downy as a baby's in the lantern's glow. Les's pecker got excited all over again.

"Well, hell," he told himself. "No sense going halfway down the trail."

He thought Buck was asleep. He freed his pecker and got behind him, but he no sooner had then Buck reached back and took hold of him. He scooted back and guided Les's dick to him. Les felt a shudder of excitement as the tip of his knob found the little hole. Damned if it wasn't greased. Hole was little, though, and pole big. He pushed, and Buck groaned.

"Don't you be complaining," Les said. "Way you been begging."

"Don't hear me begging you to quit, do you?" Buck shoved back hard at him and Les's prick slid halfway in. Jesus, that was tight. He hesitated, afraid he was paining his partner.

"I never done this before," he said.

"Me neither."

"You never took it up the ass before?"

"Not no fence post," Buck said. He twisted his little butt around and almost made Les shoot a load right there and then. "You going to fuck, or you going to lay there jabbering?"

That did it. Les shoved him over on his belly, rolling on top of him. He drove it home and began to fuck Buck in earnest. He didn't care now if it did hurt. But if Buck minded, he had a peculiar way of showing it. He could've made butter the way his butt was churning.

"How's that feel?" Buck asked breathlessly.

"It's okay," Les panted.

Buck snorted. "Liar. Just okay?"

"Son of a bitch, all right, it feels fuckin' great, you stupid bastard." For revenge, he began to ramrod Buck, pulling back until only the tip was still inside, then burying his cock to his balls, so hard that Buck gave a little woof of breath at the impact. Buck twisted all the harder and arched his back to get everything he could.

He reached for Les's hand and put it on his dick. Les had never held any cock but his own. He slid his fingers up and down, surprised at how slick it felt. Hell, maybe he'd greased that, too. It was hard as rock, though not as big as his, but nothing to be ashamed of either.

Les ground into the man, and Buck moaned with pleasure. It gave Les an odd thrill to know his dick could make somebody that happy. Yolanda's girls all moaned and groaned, but he knew instinctively Buck's pleasure was real, and that he was creating it. He felt a surge of sexual power and pride he had never known.

When the hole he was poking suddenly spasmed about his dick and his hand was all wet, he realized belatedly that Buck had come. The discovery brought him off as well, and he pumped a powerful eruption up Buck's tight hole.

They lay for several minutes, regaining their breath. Les
slipped his dick out, even though it hadn't yet gone down any.

"I guess that'll satisfy my curiosity," he said.

"Maybe you ought to take turnabout," Buck said. "If you
ain't tired. Finish your education."

"School's over," Les got up and tucked his unhappy prick
back in his trousers. "Busy day tomorrow. Best get some sleep."

Most of the week that followed, Les made it a point to avoid
Buck. When they did meet, though, Buck was strangely sub-
dued. In place of his usual tomfoolery, he'd just smile and look
down kind of shy-like. Even the other cowhands noticed something different, though they weren't sure what. Les saw them
looking at him and Buck a little curiously.

Saturday night came again, and the boys rode into town. Les
thought about Yolanda's, but he'd be embarrassed if the girls all
knew about the last time. Maybe he'd go look for a poker game
at the cantina instead. He went out to the trough by the barn
to wash up. He was only half surprised when Buck came out of
the barn.

"You might as well've gone with the boys," Les said, ignoring him and stripping off his shirt. "I'm fixing to ride into town.
By myself." He emphasized the last part.

"What about...you know? Saturday night's our night, ain't
it?"

"Our night? We ain't got no night."

"Well, you being shy, and everybody gone, seems like that's
the best time for us."

"Damn it, they ain't no us," Les said vehemently. "You get
that shit out of your head. Just 'cause I fucked you once don't
mean I'm going to again." He took a bucket and splashed water
over his back and chest.

"The trouble with you," Buck said, "is you're too damned stupid to see what we got here."

Les turned on him. "All we got here is a hot-assed half-breed who had to have my dick. Now he thinks he's gotta stick something up my ass, only that ain't never gonna happen."

"All that's making you sore," Buck said, jabbing a finger at Les's hairy chest, "is your asshole's been twitching for it since I got here and you ain't man enough to admit it."

This really riled Les, because he did have a funny kind of tingling back there that he hadn't yet put any name to. "Bastard," he swore, and swung his fist, only Buck wasn't where'd been. "Damnation," he said, and swung again, and again Buck dodged the blow.

With a roar, Les charged at him, and somehow their feet got tangled and they fell to the ground. They rolled back and forth in the dirt, punching ineffectively at each other and grunting and snarling. "Son of a bitch," someone said, and, "Cocksucker."

After a few minutes they fell apart and lay side by side, breathing heavy.

"Don't look like nobody's winnin'," Les said. They both got up, dusting themselves and feeling a little foolish.

"You're bleeding," Buck said.

"I rolled on some rocks is all."

"I'll wash you off." Buck took off his bandana and dipped it in the trough.

"I can wash my own self."

"Let me," Buck said. "I want to."

Les hesitated, and when he didn't object, Buck washed the dirt and blood off Les's thick chest.

"Buck ain't no real name," Les said, to take his mind off the hand rubbing across one copper penny.

"Buckaroo. Bastard for *vaquero*. It's William Horse, but I

always been Buck." He rubbed the other penny. "What's Les mean?"

"Sylvester." Buck laughed aloud. "What's so goddamn funny?"

"Sounds like some prissy city dude, walks funny and all."

Les laughed too, but he grew sober as Buck's hand moved slowly over his abdomen. His dick swelled.

"What I did, the other night," Les kind of stammered. "Don't that, well, don't it hurt, having that shoved up your ass?"

"At first. Feels better as it goes. Lots better."

"What if someone was to try," Les looked over Buck's shoulder, "and say he didn't like it and wanted to stop?"

"I always promise I'll take it out if it hurts."

"Do you ever? Take it out?"

"No-o-o. By the time we talk it over, they generally decide they'd just as soon I put the rest in."

Les laughed, and caught his breath as those determined fingers pulled his pecker free. *That damn traitor!* Hadn't never been so hard, so often. He could've pounded nails with the thing.

Buck looked up, and their eyes met. Les surprised both of them by suddenly grabbing hold of the man and kissing him, tentatively at first; then their mouths were grinding together, teeth scraping, bodies trying to find ways to get even closer.

"There's some new hay up in the loft," Les said when they paused for breath. "Soft as feathers."

Buck laughed deep in his throat and led him into the barn, pausing to bolt the door, case anybody came back early. There was a can of axle grease by the buckboard, and he took that with him. By the time he topped the ladder, Les was lying on the hay in his union suit, eyes closed.

"Why don't you get them long johns off?" Buck said, hastily shedding his own clothes.

"There's a trap door in the back of them."

"I got me a beautiful man in the hay, and I want to see what I got."

"Never heard no man called beautiful," Les grumbled, but he peeled the union suit off and lay back naked, dick standing tall. An owl fluttered its wings in the rafters.

Buck straddled him. "Damn it, open them eyes," he said, and when Les did, he said, "What do you see?"

Les shrugged. "A naked man," he said, and when Buck waited, he added, "With a boner." After another long moment, he said, "All right, goddamn it, a beautiful man."

Buck grinned. "Who's going to fuck you raw."

"Am I supposed to turn over, or what?"

"Why don't you just leave this to me? I'm the one knows what he's doing." He lifted Les's legs over his shoulders and reached down to grease the man's waiting hole.

"Shit!" Les exclaimed as Buck's knob forced its way in.

"You gonna be a baby, or you gonna take this like a man?"

"I reckon you can get that bitty thing in there without too much trouble," Les said, gritting his teeth.

"Fuck you," Buck told him, and he did. But he stopped and rested about halfway in to give Les time to get used to it.

Les felt like he was being split in two. Seemed like Buck's cock must have doubled in size since he'd looked at it a moment before. Buck leaned down and kissed him. After a minute or two, Les felt his butt muscles relax. Buck felt it too. He began to fuck him, slow and gentle, but he knew by instinct when the pain had turned to pleasure, and he began to fuck him harder then.

"Shit," Les said. "That's—that's..." But he didn't have words to describe it.

Buck bent further and took Les's prick into his mouth. Les

moaned with pleasure. All those different sensations: the pole plowing steadily in and out of his butt, the mouth on his knob, even the slap of balls that made his upturned ass tingle. He wanted everything all at once: to kiss Buck, to hug him fiercely, to fuck him too.

Not a puppy, he thought suddenly: a *gato montez*—a wildcat. "Ride 'em, cowboy!" he gasped. He raised his ass and hugged Buck even closer.

Something changed. Buck's prick swelled enormously and exploded, and Les realized that Buck was firing a load up his ass. Knowing it made his cock go off, spurt after spurt. Buck choked and swallowed furiously—but the fucker never spilled a drop.

They lay locked together for a while. "Got to drive them longhorns up to Wichita," Les said. "You fixing to come along?"

Buck kissed him. "Darlin'," he said, "ain't you figured out yet about you and me?" And, just like that, damned if Les's prick wasn't standing at attention again. Buck slid down and began to suck on it. He paused to say, "I like it regular."

"I reckon you won't suffer none," Les said flatly. After another moment, he added, "You think the boys'll guess? About us?"

Buck snickered. "You damn fool, them boys been taking bets."

Les snorted and gave Buck's head a push. "If you're gonna suck, suck. You can jaw anytime." Buck obeyed enthusiastically.

Darlin', Les thought. Nobody'd ever called him that before. He rolled the word around on his tongue, savoring it. He lifted his head and looked down, realizing how ripe and kissable Buck's lips were, cock bruised and berry red by now. He hadn't ever kissed nobody either. He wished Buck could kiss him and suck him at the same time.

Just now, though, sucking took precedence. He gave Buck's head another shove, case Buck might want to take it a little deeper. He did. Les sighed happily.

"One thing's sure," Les said. "My bedroll's gonna be a lot less lonesome."

THE PICKUP MAN

Shane Allison

'm relieved I'm able to make it to Billy's in my piece-of-shit car. It crackles over rock and gravel as I make my way into the parking lot. A week ago it wouldn't start when I was leaving the baths. The last thing I wanted was to call my dad to tell him the carburetor was acting up again and he'd have to pick me up from a bathhouse. He's already embarrassed that I can't tell a flat tire from a dead battery. What can I say? All I know how to do is put gas in 'em and drive 'em.

When I open the thick wooden door, Lynard Skynard blasts out of the hole-in-the-wall country-western bar that's on the ass end of Tallahassee. It's a popular spot for local rednecks, not to mention a slew of cops who get called at least twice a week to break up a fight between a couple of drunken hicks. When I enter, I get more than a few stares, all eyes dead set on burning a hole the size of Florida clean through me.

The place reeks of stale beer and prejudice. I carefully tear past grungy denim-clad cowboys with bloodshot eyes to make my way to the bar. I sandwich myself tightly between two drunkards nursing a couple of longnecks. They look me over disgustedly, as if I don't belong there. And to be honest, Billy's is the last joint I want my black ass to be caught dead in. I stick out like a sore thumb in my Timberlands and baggy FUBUs. I wait and watch the burly bartender pop tops off bottles of cold German beer before I wave him down. He gives me a stern glare. I yell through the brash country tunes roaring from the jukebox that sits against a wall of cinder blocks, "Excuse me. Where's your bathroom?" I hold out my oil-soiled hands. He points past ten-gallon-hooded heads to the far end of the bar. I saunter past mean, prying eyes that continue to watch me as if I'm going to magically sprout wings from my ass.

I press the door open to the men's room where a bunch of cowboys stand side by side at the urinal trough. My dick twitches in my baggy jeans to the sizzle of piss splashing against the glossy porcelain. Some turn to take a look at the new addition; others focus on emptying their bladders. At the sink, I turn the tap with the side of my hand, careful not to smudge it with oil. Cowboy after cowboy enters the shitter, each with a dick full of piss. I'm a bundle of nerves in this den of country boys. I press pink liquid soap into my dirty palms and work it into a frantic lather.

My dick gets thick as I gawk at the row of tight, redneck booties flexing and farting in jeans. I rinse the soap off my hands as I run them under a tongue of cold water. I stare at these muscular, big-butt cowboys as streams of gold shower the trough. I gotta pee so bad I'm about to explode—I've been holding it in since I left home, thinking I could wait until I got to Brian's party. A space opens up between two guys, and I quickly elbow my way between them. "Sorry," I tell them, as I take my place alongside their flannel-clad bear bodies.

As I unzip and fish my dick out of my underwear, I nonchalantly take a peek at soft peckers the size of Vienna sausages being shaken clean of pee. Others are fully erect with cockheads of all shapes and sizes. Some have the typical mushroom head while others are simply cloaked in tender pink foreskin. Some dicks are riddled with veins; others look sweaty and ripe from being held captive in briefs all day. Some even sport Prince Albert crowns. I want nothing more than to drop to my knees and worship each and every erection in all its glory.

I feel a slight burn as I make my own donation into the golden river. I watch for prying eyes to see if any of these country ruffians are checking out my equipment. I'm not what you'd call "porn-star big," but I hold my own, and the boys don't complain. I don't care if they're looking. I'm a dirty little exhibitionist anyway. *Like what you see?* I think. Several of the men have come and gone and have hauled out into a vortex of Brooks and Dunn vibrating against paneled walls and the shoddy Sheetrocked ceiling.

There are only three of us left draining the last droplets from the slits of our dicks. A short, pudgy Mexican dude wearing a cream-colored cowboy hat and caramel-brown boots has finished up, tucking his uncut dick into a tomb of boxers. The medium-build guy to the right of me wears a red and black long-sleeve flannel shirt, a gray cowboy hat, and faded jeans with holes in the knees. He's got a round, bubble, black-boy booty that's firm in dirty denim. His dick is cut, the head slightly freckled. We stand together, close as any two men can get, each playing with ourself for the other to see. I watch excitedly as his dirty fingers squeeze his curved dick.

Just when he's about to grab my cock, two men walk in and take their places next to us. The cowboy nervously puts away his boner and saunters to a vacant sink to wash up. I swaddle my sex back into my Hanes and duck into a stall that's filled with wads of wet toilet paper and soggy cigarette butts. I unroll some tissue and try to clean the toilet rim of pee and what can only be described as tobacco that has been spewed from the dirtiest mouth in town.

A hole's been gutted in the wall of the stall to the left of me. The partition is caked with mostly racist and homophobic graffiti: NIGGERS GO HOME and DIE STALL FAGS. An intricate picture of a Confederate flag has been drawn above the glory hole. The best part of public shitters is reading the ridiculous messages guys scribble while they're pinching a loaf. Some people have way too much time on their hands. I'm one to talk, though, since I'm guilty of sprawling my own dirty messages across bathroom walls.

I push my jeans around my knees to keep them from dragging across the disgusting floor. As I hear the heels of the cowboy's boots against the tile, I stoop over to watch a pair of cruddy snakeskins make their way into the stall next to mine. My glasses graze against the partition. I take them off and stuff them into my shirt pocket. I play with myself as I watch him undress from the waist down. He takes his dick out, then wraps his fingers around it, giving me a state-of-the-art glory-hole show. I glide my index finger within the circle, letting him know I hunger for what hangs between his thick, hairy thighs.

I watch as his crotch comes through the hole. I tilt the soft-hanging member under my nose to give it my infamous smell test. I approve, and work the rest of it past my lips and into my warmth mouth. My tongue slithers along the belly of his snake. The traffic from new visitors is thick, but we're both locked securely in our stalls. Some piss and leave, while others linger, as if they know what's up. I struggle to keep my slurping to a minimum by wrapping my lips tighter around his stuff.

Suddenly he uncorks his dick from my mouth. With traces of drool at the corners of my yapper, I watch for his next move. "Let's go back to my truck," he whispers through the hole, his breath reeking of booze. I make out a coarse brown mustache that covers his top lip. We hurry to make ourselves decent, so much so that my dick nearly catches in the copper jaws of my zipper. When I exit the stall, there's a new row of bodacious cowboys taking leaks, but I couldn't care less.

My dick guides me past a school of pool-playing, beer-guzzling men and into a poorly lit lot of cars, jeeps, and dirty four-by-fours. Whether my crappy car will crank or not is the last thing on my mind. I turn the corner of a green Dumpster to find a pickup near the fence with its parking lights on. It's caked with dried mud. I walk to the front of the truck. THE PICKUP MAN is painted in neat letters across the top of the windshield. I try to make out the cowboy's face through his dark-tinted windows. He pushes open the passenger-side door, but I'm hesitant to get in: I don't know this guy from Adam, and his truck reeks of dead deer.

"How's it goin'?" I ask.

"Hey," he replies. It's dark in the parking lot, but I can make out some of his features.

"That was hot back there," I tell him, even though I'm a bit uneasy about all this. Suddenly I feel like a fly in this dude's web, thinking maybe he's out to spill a punk's blood and leave me for dead in a ditch off some lonely highway. *Don't be stupid,* I think.

"I know a place we can go," he says gruffly.

I usually don't get into cars with guys I don't know—especially guys driving big-ass pickups with tinted windows—but he's a piece of ass too good to pass up. When guys start talking about going back to their place, I usually change my mind and get the hell outta Dodge. Cars with tinted windows really freak me out. A month ago, a local girl was raped and sodomized after she accepted a ride from a stranger. Cops describe the vehicle as a white van with blue stripes and dark windows. They still haven't found the bastard.

"I don't know about going anywhere," I tell him. I look around nervously to study my surroundings just in case this guy tries to kidnap my ass.

"It's cool. I ain't weird or nothin'," he tells me.

After careful consideration, I make up my mind to go along, and I climb into the cab of his pickup. Besides, I have a switch-blade in case this motherfucker wants to kick up some shit. I don't want to have to cut a bitch, but I will if things get critical. "Lead the way," I tell him. My heart beats heavy as his truck bucks slowly out of the lot. He drives farther and farther out of the clutches of the city limits, past greasy spoons and signs with store names that end in "4 Less."

"So where we goin'?" I ask him.

"There's a rest stop off Highway 10," he says. "Don't worry. We're almost there."

The pickup roars like a mythical beast as he presses deep into the gas, making his way down a dirt road that slices apart a wooded area off the bustling freeway. There are a few cars in sight, and the ruffian jostles his pickup between two of them, neither of which is occupied by the drivers.

"Dude, is this safe?" I ask.

"It's pretty quiet 'round this time of night. Come on. Let's go in back." He lets down the tail end of the truck exposing the bed strewn with tools and sawed-off pieces of paneling. I press the knife in my pocket, ready to pull it out in case he tries anything. I can't help thinking of the van-driving rapist. "Hop in," he says. "Just push some of this shit off to the side."

As I crawl in on my knees, pushing junk out of the way, he grabs my ass and presses a finger in the crevice of my butt. He climbs in behind me and collapses into a nest of heavy, hard things that pushes into our flesh. He takes off his cowboy hat and tosses it inside the truck on the seat. Feathers of sweaty black hair are exposed, along with a touch of gray in his brows. His pot roast of a gut is snug under his T-shirt, which displays a pit bull bearing its teeth beneath a Confederate flag. His nipples are pert under the cotton. Like erasers, these things. His big metal belt buckle hangs limply from his waist as he unzips his Wranglers. I watch as he pulls the snakeskin boots off his tube sock–covered feet. "Aintcha gonna get undressed?" he asks.

"I don't know about this, man. Somebody might see us out here."

"It's cool," he assures me. "Nobody'll fuck with us."

He starts to unbutton my shirt with his gritty fingers. It doesn't take me long to get out of my clothes. We're both still in our socks and underwear when he asks me what I'm into.

"Well, you already know I like to suck," I tell him. "I'm pretty versatile, really. I'll try almost anything once."

He reaches into the cotton crotch panel of his briefs and pulls out the dick I'd worshiped a short while ago in the crapper at Billy's. "Anything, huh?" he says. He peels his briefs off hulking legs and tosses them in a nowhere-special direction. A salt-and-pepper thicket surrounds his horse-hung erection. Compared to this rough, redneck of a thing, I have nothing much to offer between my legs.

When I move in to give his nipples a taste test, the congestion in the bed of his truck shuffles beneath my bare, black ass. They blush as I bite and suck them with love. "Ow, fuck!" he yells.

I move between his thighs and take his dick in my nervous palm. His ball sac is tender and coarse. He runs his hands through the kinky crop of my hair as I manhandle his nipples. "Suck me, boy," he demands, pushing me with force past his beer belly. I waste no time putting his dick in my mouth. I nuzzle my nose in his nest of cowboy-crotch stink. "Awesome, man!" he says. "You suck purty good."

His calling me "boy" gets me hot, causing my dick to thicken even more as I struggle not to gag on his sex. I want him to know I can take a dick proper like a good boy. We turn our bodies in a sixty-nine position. He spreads his legs as I lick along the shaft and suckle the tender goose-bump flesh of his sac. His sweaty hair is cold against the inside of my thigh as he devours my cock. His teeth graze against it, but what's hot sex without a little pain? I brace myself each time his choppers skim along my dick.

"Roll on over, boy. On your back," he says.

My knees point up to the stars as he services me with unrelenting fervor. I squeeze his booty as he runs my dick in and out of his mouth again. He's ripe and sweaty as I glide my tongue along his cherry. "Oh, man, that's awesome. Do that," he says.

He leisurely works his burly butt upon the throne of my face. *There you are, Daddy,* I think, tongue-tickling his button. His dick grazes my chest as I munch away on his butt. The tip of my ring finger slides in easily up his wet stuff. I'm careful not to damage his goods, for his butt is as precious to me as the night sky. I lick and spit continuously on the cowboy's sphincter, fucking him with four fingers, which go up him without a hitch.

"You wanna fuck me, boy?" I'm too busy with his backside to answer. "I wanna fuck."

"You got a rubber?" I ask him.

The cowboy grabs the leg of his jeans and drags them toward our nude bodies. He feels around in one of the pockets and pulls out a cellophane packet. He tears it with his teeth then uses his mouth to roll the prophylactic over my sex. He pulls his cheeks apart with calloused, cruddy fingers, and my dick slides easily up his country ass. In amazement I watch as his walls gorge on my dick.

"Oh, man that's it," he announces. I claw his butt as he rides me like one of those mechanical bulls back at Billy's. Beads of sweat trickle from his furry back as I thrust my sex up his butt with wild abandon. "God, fuck!" he yells.

I never thought I was that great at fucking, but with all the cursing and fussing this hick is doing, I guess I'm not as bad as I thought. I give him a reach around, tugging on his dick like a cow's udder. "Yeah, like that," he says. "I'm close."

The screwing and jerking is in perfect synchronization. "Let's nut together," I tell him.

His moans are sweet music to my ears. "Um comin'," he announces.

You and me both. When I expectedly feel something warm between my fingers, I tug his dick, milking him of every drop. My breaths are heavy; my gluteus maximus muscles ache and burn. I yell silently in my dirty mind that I'm about to come. I brace against his bear shoulders as I climax up his ass, into the flesh-colored rubber. My body relaxes as he slides off my cock.

"You sure can fuck," he says breathlessly.

With aching muscles, we rest for a while before getting dressed. I slap him on the butt as he pushes a foot into one of his boots. When we climb back into the cab, the windshield has fogged with the night's cold. He wipes it clear and drives me back to Billy's, where the graveled lot is empty except for my car parked on the side of the bar.

He pulls in front of Spears Seafood, where they have a sale on roe and oysters, and asks if we could get together again. I scribble my cell number on the back of an old grocery receipt.

His 'stache pricks my face when he leans over and kisses me on the cheek.

My car stalls a few times but successfully cranks up after the fourth attempt. "Thank you, baby," I say, kissing its steering wheel.

I'm not even home yet before my cell phone rings.

"Hello?"

"Hey." It's the cowboy. "I forgot to tell ya I had a good time."

I laugh and assure him that I, too, had fun. We make a date to meet at a bar-and-grill place that's a tad classier than Billy's. I get home and collapse on the bed with his cowboy-bear scent on me like cheap cologne.

BUNKHOUSE ORGY

Bearmuffin

Things were Spartan for cowboys working at the Q Ranch. After riding hard from sunup to sundown, all they had to look forward to was a drafty, dusty bunkhouse equipped with rock-hard wooden beds and thin cotton mattresses, and not much else.

Well, there was a little more to it than that.

A cowboy can get as lonesome as a preacher on pay night, and after a couple of months out in the sage on a long, hard cattle drive there's more comforting to be had than just a hot cock down your throat or up your ass.

That's when things got wild at the bunkhouse. Shane Rawlins was back at the ranch, horny as hell and ready for action. A greenhorn from Reno, Nevada, he had curly black hair, sparkling green eyes, and a radiant smile. He was a tower of rippling muscle with a magnificent torso and a V-shaped back. His perfect, hard bubble butt made the other ranch hands' mouths drop open. He sported a thick ten-inch cock and a pair of awesome low-hangers.

It was Shane's first time at the Q Ranch, so he hadn't yet met his bunkmates. His heart pounding with anticipation, he rode up to the bunkhouse. He dismounted his horse and stepped up to the door. It was wide open.

Crumpled beer cans, cotton briefs, and dusty jeans were strewn on the floor. A grimy pair of briefs lying on the bed caught Shane's eye. He picked them up and held them to his face. The unmistakable musky smell of man rushed up his nose. Shockwaves of lust shot to his groin as he thought of hefty cock and massive balls trapped inside the fabric.

Shane reeled from the briefs' hot stench. He put them down before he shot his load and stepped over to the fridge to get a beer. He was about to pick up a brew when he felt a strong tug on his jeans and spun around. It was Colt Stevens, a cowboy from Nebraska.

Shane's heart leapt to his throat. He was riveted to his spot. Colt was a muscled giant with crew-cut blond hair and steel-blue eyes. Shane's eyes were glued to Colt's wide chest and thick, rounded biceps.

The six-foot-three cowboy was completely naked except for cowboy boots, a dirty jockstrap, and brown leather chaps. Shane was transfixed by Colt's bulging jock pouch. A big hole exposed two inches of thick, blue-veined cock that made Shane's mouth water.

"You horny?" Colt grunted.

"Sure am." Shane was impressed with Colt's rugged good looks, firm chin, and sensuous lips. He grabbed his own crotch and gave it a good squeeze.

Colt was excited by the sight of Shane clad in a tight blue button-up shirt and faded Wranglers. The jeans were slung low

over Shane's hips, exposing the upper half of his bright red boxers. He felt his cock jump inside his jock.

"Let's get comfortable," Colt said. Shane eagerly responded
to the suggestion and shucked off his clothes, as did Colt.

Colt ogled Shane, his eyes narrowing to two slits, as he took
in every inch of his muscular, perfectly proportioned body. He
ran his tongue over his lips.

Colt wasted no time. He dropped to his knees behind Shane
and spread the man's buttocks wide open. "I gotta lick your
ass," he said, and pushed his tanned face into Shane's cheeks.

First, Colt broad-stroked Shane's buttocks with his rough
tongue. Then he darted into his musky ass crack. Shane shuddered, wiggling his butt from side to side. He felt his butt hairs
glide along Colt's flicking tongue. Shane heard Colt's grunts,
his choked moans of lust. The cowboy nuzzled his face against
Shane's sweet butthole and greedily sucked up his sweaty butt
juices. Then *wham!* Colt's tongue landed right on Shane's butt
bud. "Yeah," Shane moaned, lusty shivers running along his
spine. "Suck my hole," he hissed, thrusting his butt against
Colt's invading tongue.

Gluing his mouth to Shane's butthole, Colt buried his nose
in the fine, golden ass hairs sprouting around Shane's butthole.
Then he stuck his thick, hot tongue up Shane's bunghole. "Fuck,
yeah. Suck my hole," Shane said, enjoying the fantastic sensation of Colt's rough tongue wiggling inside his hole.

Suddenly, Brody Hughes burst into the bunkhouse. A wild
grin creased his rugged face. Brody was a ranch hand from Wyoming, and Colt was his fuckbuddy.

Shane stared at Brody's 210 pounds of lean, hard muscle
packed on his six-foot-two frame. The redheaded cowboy wore
a faded Levi's jacket over a tight T-shirt cut just above his navel, revealing an impressive set of rock-hard abs. Tufts of black

pubic hair curled over the waistband of his white cotton briefs that were exposed by his low-slung 501s. His boots were caked with dried mud.

Brody tromped over to the fridge and grabbed a beer. He popped it open and watched incredulously as Colt pushed Shane to the floor and straddled him, planting his butt squarely on Shane's surprised face. "Eat my ass," he said. Shane smiled. He was more than ready to chow down on some hot, sweaty cowboy butt.

Brody's powerful, square jaw hit the floor. His coal-black eyes opened wide with amazement. Fuck! His buddy was getting rimmed! Brody quickly stripped to his skivvies. His cock bolted up and pushed through the pee-flap, its head sticking out lewdly. With a savage glint in his eyes, he shucked off his briefs. Brody's fat pisser quivered violently. Thick salty drops of pre-cum dripped from his pisshole and trickled to the floor, forming a puddle between his toes.

Brody knelt and forced himself between Shane's muscular legs. He lifted Shane's calves and pitched them across his brawny shoulders. Then the hairy cowboy reached under to grab Shane's sweat-slicked buns and wrenched them wide apart. With a lusty growl, he positioned the blunt tip of his precum-drooling cock against Shane's quivering butthole.

Brody's fingers squeezed Shane's ripe buttocks. "Fuck," Brody snorted. "Nice firm buns, stud!" With a hearty grunt he sliced into Shane's ass. Shane grimaced with pain when he felt Brody's spasming cock glide up his tight asshole.

"Awwww, fuck!" Shane cried out. But the pain soon grew into pleasurable waves of lust. He clenched his bunghole around Brody's pumping cock.

"Like my cock, huh?" Brody grunted thickly. He sloshed his bulldong in and out of Shane's slick asshole.

"Fuck me, stud," Shane begged. "Fuck me with your big, hard cock!"

While Brody brutally ass-fucked Shane, Colt tightened his massive tree-trunk thighs around Shane's head and grinned lecherously. He mashed his butthole against Shane's fluttering tongue. "Eat my ass. Eat it!" Colt shouted. Shane licked the blond hairs swirling around Colt's musky hole. He thrust his tongue inside Colt's butt and twirled it around and around. Colt moaned and squatted down even harder on Shane's probing tongue. Shane glued his mouth around Colt's butthole and sucked it inside out.

Colt howled like a maniac. "AWWWW FUUUCK!" he screamed, fisting his cock. Thick drops of precum seeped from his pisshole. "Eat it stud. EAT MY HOLE!"

Brody continued to plow Shane's asshole with his massive cock. After Shane had totally rimmed Colt's ass, Colt was ready for a blow job. He grabbed Shane's head and held it steady as he forced his spasming cock down Shane's throat. At first Shane gagged and moaned, but then he sucked in his cheeks and took Colt's bloated cock all the way down his throat. His tongue fluttered up and down beneath Colt's throbbing prick.

"Suck it!" Colt panted. "SUCK MY COCK!"

Shane gasped for air. His mouth was stuffed to bursting with Colt's beefy rod. Shane let Colt's cock slide out of his mouth to take a few quick breaths. But Colt couldn't wait to mount Shane's face again and stuff his huge balls down the struggling cowboy's mouth.

Colt ran his hands over Shane's muscular pecs, kneading the hard golden-tanned flesh between his sturdy hands. He grabbed Shane's nipples and gave them a hearty pull. Shane moaned, his body shuddering with each tug on his tender nipples. He sucked Colt's fat balls into his mouth and slurped noisily on them.

"Awwwww, fuck!" Colt cried out. "Suck my balls, stud. SUCK 'EM!"

Colt reached for Brody's thick nipples. He grabbed the tips and dug his nails into them.

Brody screamed, "ARRRRGH! FUUUUUCK!" Shane felt Brody's cock expand inside him. Brody plowed deeper and deeper until his hairy nuts crashed against Shane's swollen balls. Colt hunched forward and sucked Brody's licker into his hungry mouth. Hot spit bubbles dribbled down their mouths as they exchanged a long, hot kiss.

Brody's cock swelled inside Shane, totally filling his asshole. It felt like a hot water pipe ready to burst. Yeah, Brody's cock was ready to explode!

"FUUUCKK!" Brody howled. "GONNA SHOOT. GONNA FUCKIN' SHOOT!"

Shane looked up at Colt. His eyes were wide open, his handsome face filled with lust. "AWWWW FUUUCK, AWWWW FUUUCK!" Colt cried. His mouth twitched, his body shuddered, and hot sweat streamed over his muscles. He whipped his head from side to side.

"Want my load?" Colt said.

"Yeah," Shane rasped. "Give it to me!"

"Hold on, Colt," Brody growled. "I'm gonna squirt!"

Colt bellowed as he drove his cock down Shane's spasming throat. Shane writhed helplessly as Colt's hot, frothing cum blasted over his tongue and rushed down his throat.

"FUUUUUUUUCCCKKKK!" Brody howled. He smashed into Shane's butt, sinking his hot bullcock to the very root. A fountain of foaming white jizz sprayed from Brody's wide pisshole, filling Shane's asshole like lava. Shane's sweat-soaked body shuddered violently as he gurgled and choked on the hot cum dribbling from the corners of his swollen mouth. His sore asshole spasmed as Brody's bulljizz slowly trickled out.

"The fridge is full of cold beer, and we're hornier than hell," Colt said. "Think you can handle an all-nighter?"

Shane's cock jerked lustily at the prospect of more fucking and sucking with the two cowboys.

"Yeehaw!" Shane cried, thinking Colt and Brody sure knew how to welcome a stud to the Q Ranch.

PONY EXPRESS

Vic Winter

t's imperative this letter get through," Dawson said as he handed Zeke a thick vellum envelope with neat, square writing on
it: COLONEL WILMINGTON, FORT WASHINGTON.

Johnny Samuels tried to grab the letter from him. He always
wanted the next run, even when it wasn't his turn. His grubby
hands didn't even touch the fine paper, though. "*Imperative*
means it's real important, Ezekiel," Johnny told him.

Zeke rolled his eyes and put the letter in his mailbag. He
knew what the word meant. The mail always had to go through.
If Dawson said it was imperative, it just meant there'd be trouble
if he didn't get the letter to its destination.

"The outlaws have been attacking all manner of folk lately,"
Dawson said. "Been worse than them Indians. But you get as
far as Lonesome Pass and Tom'll meet you there with a fresh
horse. He's got a couple of soldiers with him, help you get to
Fort Washington."

Zeke nodded at Dawson and donned his hat and gloves. "I'll get her through, boss."

"I know you will."

He shook Dawson's hand, like he always did, and eagerly mounted Lightning. There was nothing he liked better than riding—well, almost nothing. He smiled, thinking of Tom up at Lonesome Pass. Even the recent attacks on the Pony Express couldn't curb his enthusiasm.

He made sure his mailbag and canteen were securely over his shoulder, put his bandana up over his mouth and nose, and grabbed the reins. "Come on, Lightning," he said. "Gotta live up to your name again."

Soon they were at the edge of town, and it didn't take any time at all before they'd left the buildings behind them, and it was just Zeke and his horse, kicking up dust as they pounded over the dry trail. The sun sat high in the sky, bright and hot, and Zeke flowed with Lightning, his body rocking as they galloped. He could do this in his sleep, he thought—even had once or twice.

He didn't stop to eat, but he did slow a little as he pulled some jerky out of his bag and chewed off a piece. He should have known better, because that's when the shooting started. There was a distant bang and a buzz, just past his ears.

"Shit!" He dropped his jerky and adjusted the reigns real quick, sliding to one side as he hugged Lightning's body, making himself as small a target as possible. He didn't need to do anything to get Lightning to go full out. If that first bullet hadn't been enough to do it, the next two would have been.

Lightning ran fast as a horse could, Zeke clinging tight with his legs, thighs gripping hard as Lightning's hooves beat a rapid tattoo.

Zeke's luck held. The outlaws were far enough away that

they had no real hope of hitting him and didn't bother giving chase. Of course, by the time Zeke had outrun the shooting, his heart was pumping so hard his blood was going through his veins faster than Lightning could run.

Lathered in sweat, Lightning's sides heaved as he kept moving, and Zeke thanked God they didn't have much farther to go before Lonesome Pass. The high cliffs offered shade and some shelter, but at the same time it made for easy pickings if someone had a mind to shoot you—there was nowhere to go and the Pony Express outpost was little more than a stable with a roof and one rock wall.

Zeke heard a shout as he pushed Lightning to keep going. It was Tom's voice carrying on the dry air. "Rider coming in!"

"Pony rider!" Zeke called back, letting Tom and whoever was with him know he wasn't an outlaw.

The shooting started again as soon as he'd called out, bullets zinging by his ears, a heck of a lot closer this time. Zeke flattened himself against Lightning's back and held on as those hooves picked up speed again.

As they flew into the stable, Lightning nearly running into the rock wall, a soldier popped up right behind him and fired in the direction Zeke had just come from. Zeke was breathing nearly as hard as Lightning, and he was nearly as wet, too, sweat dripping into his eyes as he slid off Lightning's back.

Hands pulled him down into a small space beneath a bench, and he curled up with Tom, wincing as bullets flew past him.

"Lightning gonna be okay out there?"

"Don't know, Zeke. Gotta trust he ain't gonna get hit because no way is he gonna fit down here with us."

Zeke nodded and tried to grin, but it turned into a grimace as a bullet hit the rock by Lightning's head. Zeke wriggled out, Tom's fingers grasping at him, trying to keep him beneath the bench. "Just a sec," he growled, leaning up far enough to grab Lightning's reins. "Come on, boy. Lie down now. You'll be safer. Come on."

Lightning reared up, eyes rolling, but then let Zeke pull him down. Nostrils flaring, Lightning whinnied and shook his head. Zeke petted his forehead. "Just stay down, boy. It'll be okay."

He let Tom's hands pull him back under the bench and met his worried green eyes under a thatch of red curls. It made Zeke grin to see those messy curls. Tom was always in need of a haircut and today was no different. He pushed them out of the way and patted Tom's head.

"I'm all right. And now Lightning is too. Where's the other horses?"

"Back at the other end of the pass with the other soldier. Nobody's shooting that end." Tom's voice was soft, and he reached out a hand, wiping dirt from just above Zeke's nose. "You're a mess."

Zeke nodded. "I had to ride hard. This isn't the first time I been shot at today."

Tom's eyes widened, and Zeke was pulled close to the lean body, the freckles across Tom's nose standing out as his face paled a bit.

Zeke kept petting. "'S all right, Tommy. I ain't got shot, right?"

"Not yet."

Zeke just grinned, another bullet hitting the rock face above them, making his body vibrate with the sound and what it meant. "Nope. Not yet."

"Let's keep it that way."

Zeke nodded and pressed closer against Tom, their bodies touching from necks to boots. Zeke felt a rush of something that had nothing to do with being shot at go through him, and he pressed his lips to Tom's, the kiss hard but not nearly as quick as he'd meant to make it.

"Zeke."

"What?" Like he didn't know.

"We said we weren't gonna do that no more."

"You want me to stop?"

Tom was quiet so long that Zeke thought maybe he did want him to stop, that this time was the time Tom would actually back away and stand firm. But then those green eyes went dark, and Tom pressed his mouth to Zeke's again, kissing him hard enough his lip split on his teeth.

Moaning, Zeke started humping against Tom, licking his way into his mouth, fucking it with his tongue like there was no tomorrow. Which, considering the bullets flying past them, maybe there wasn't.

Tom was still and silent, letting him do what he wanted, and Zeke was desperate enough to let that be enough. Then, without warning, the body against his came alive, Tom rubbing back against him, his hand sliding to undo the buttons on Zeke's trousers, finding his cock, and wrapping around it.

Zeke cried out, and suddenly it was Tom's tongue fucking his mouth, that hand working him just like he needed, holding his flesh tight and stroking good and hard. He wormed his own hand into Tom's pants, just sort of holding the hard prick he found there, too far gone to give back properly at the moment.

It didn't take long, the danger, the heat, even the dust making it all too much, and Zeke groaned as he spent, heat spilling up over Tom's hand, making the space between them smell like sex.

For a moment, Zeke's body went lax, but Tom still kissed him hard, and he got the message. He tugged on Tom's cock, the hot silky skin sliding along his palm, the rough cotton of Tom's uniform against the back of his hand. He'd held his own cock plenty, but he'd never felt anything as fine as Tom's cock and it made him go hard again.

He grabbed hold of Tom's tongue with his lips, sucking hard as his hand worked that pretty cock, wanting Tom to feel as good as he did. Tom moved like a racehorse against him, his body pushing that hot prick through Zeke's hand. Tom was almost as quick off the mark as he'd been, cock throbbing, the head expanding and getting so hard, and then the smell of sex grew stronger as heat flowed over Zeke's hand.

They lay collapsed together, breathing each other in, Zeke turning it into a soft kiss every time another bullet shot near them. The bullets were coming less frequently now, though, and Tom nudged him. "Best get cleaned up, Zeke. 'Fore anyone notices."

Zeke kissed Tom one last time, then nodded, putting a little space between them so he could wipe his messy hands in the dirt and do up his pants.

Tom did the same, making a face. "We look like we been to the cathouse."

Zeke took a good look at Tom, liking the way Tom's lips were kind of swollen from their kissing. He reached out and smudged some dirt at the corner of the soldier's lips, then shook his head. "Nope. We look like we've been hiding in the dirt, hoping we don't get killed."

The bullets had stopped, and the other soldier called to them. "You boys still in one piece back there?"

"Yes, sir," Tom yelled back.

"All right, Tom. Grab your horse and get down to Jefferson. I'll follow soon as I know the shooting's done."

They crawled out from under the bench, and Zeke thought they were a right mess, both of them covered in dirt. He tugged

Lightning up, the horse still wet. "You give him a good wipe-down for me?"

"Yeah, I can do that. I got Silver Penny for you to ride on to Fort Washington with. He's good and rested." Tom stopped him a moment. "We shouldn't do this again," he said, just like he always did.

Zeke nodded, just like he always did.

They made it to the other end of the pass without any trouble, and Zeke climbed onto Silver Penny, checking to make sure he still had the letter safe in his mailbag, thinking maybe he should have checked that sooner. It was there, though, so he closed his bag back up, took a long drink from his canteen, and settled in, taking hold of the reigns.

"Good luck," murmured Tom, and Zeke nodded at him. "Ride like the wind."

"I will. See you around, Tommy."

Zeke adjusted his hat and pulled his bandana back up over his mouth and nose. He kicked his feet, and off he went, low over Silver Penny's back, the thump of the horse's hooves the only sound.

DAYLIGHT'S BURNING

Dallas Coleman

Certain folks deserved to die slow painful deaths: anyone who fed the horses spoiled feed to give 'em colic, any asshole who worked up at the bank, any jackass that would give a sixteen-year-old a new Mustang. Top of Terrell's list right now was a rude bastard who'd called his cell from an unknown number at…Christ…3:15 A.M. After he'd been drinking.

"You'd better be dyin', whoever you are."

"Shit, you ain't no nicer than you ever been, Terr. See if I call you again to let you know I'm driving through."

Well, he'd be damned. "Darrell McBride. Lord, son. Don't you know what time it is?"

Terrell rubbed his eyes a little as he sat up, back and neck creaking like old tack. Lord, he was fuzzy as shit.

"Yeah. I know," Darrell said. "I got to be in Mesquite at two. Reckoned I'd drive straight through, but I needed gas, and hell, Terr, I just got a wild hair to call. You wanna come out and have a cup of coffee or something?"

Terrell's belly went tight as a fence wire, and he nodded, near doubling over with it. Yeah. *Or something.* With them, it was always *something.* Shit. "Sure, cowboy. You over at the truck stop?"

"Yeah. I got me a room and everything. I'll order us both a cup."

"Gimme ten and I'll be there." Terrell slapped his cell phone shut and fumbled through the piles of Wranglers on the floor to find the one that wasn't walking on its own. Christ, he needed to go make eyes at Aunt Lonnie, see if she wouldn't take pity on a man and run him a couple loads of jeans. He tugged them on and grabbed his boots with his toes as he ran the shaver over his jaw. Not that he was gonna shave real good, or open the Old Spice, for Darrell, but he'd take the bristles off and brush his teeth, just in case someone saw him.

His mama hadn't raised no scum.

He still had two shirts in dry-cleaning bags and a brand-new undershirt, so he was gold, buttoning with one hand as he shoved his wallet in his back pocket with the other. "Molly, Winchester, y'all watch the trailer. I'll be back in time for kibbles."

Two tails thumped, Molly's saggy ol' bloodhound eyes opening long enough for Winchester to fart and roll over, the damn mutt trying to kill them all. Right. That was Terrell's cue to get the hell out.

There wasn't a hint of traffic on I-30, barring the semis barreling along, and even the truck stop was real quiet. 'Course, it was a Tuesday, wasn't it, and most decent folk were either sleeping the sleep of the righteous or filling their Mr. Coffees and thinking about getting to work. Darrell's Chevy was new; Terrell wouldn't have known it was his, except for that ol' trailer hooked up to it. Cowboy must be doing okay for himself, to afford that big thing.

Terrell settled his cap down solid and headed in. He wasn't gonna spend good time thinking on what was and what wasn't. Not all of them were made for busting ass on the back of a half-mad critter. Some folks had a home, damn it, family. Kids. A boss and shit. A life...

Darrell stood up from the smoking section, Stetson hanging from the hook beside the booth, black eyes shining like buttons, face tanned as good as leather, shit-eating grin twisted where the Marlboro dangled from it. Goddamn. Hell, yeah. So fine.

"I'll be damned." Darrell grinned. "Look what the cat dragged in." A big ol' hand took Terrell's and shook it good and firm.

"I swear, Anderson, you got yourself a deal with the devil, to stay looking twenty."

"You know it, son. Clean living and shit'll age you every time."

They sat, boots shuffling a little before they each found their spots, the dark brown cups already filled and steaming, a plate of eggs and toast three-quarters ate up on the table. "Well, then, you're fucking safe, Terr. You'll be kill 'em dead pretty in the grave."

Oh, yeah. Pretty. Him. "You know it, you homely bastard," Terrell grinned. So how's the circuit treating you, cowboy?"

"Good. Real good. I'm looking toward Vegas, right enough. You still roofing?"

"Doin' drywall and shit for Adam and Pete," Terrell said. "They're twins from down the road. Bought out Buck after that heart attack." He grabbed his coffee and drank deep, knowing Darrell didn't give a flying fuck about Buck or Adam or what he was doing with his days. Hell, he knew Darrell like he knew his own hands. Everything was the next ride with that boy. "Coffee's good."

"Well, it ain't Coors, but I can't get that this time of night."

Darrell was just watching him, staring into him like he had IDJIT tattooed on his forehead, or AGGIE, which'd be worse. It made him itch, made his balls crawl up and twist some. Made him hard as Chinese algebra. Bastard.

"I'm thinking beer ain't what you were hunting in this neck of the woods," Terrell said. No sense playing cat and mouse. If Darrell intended to make Mesquite in the afternoon, the man would need to be on the road by eight, and if Terrell didn't feed the mutts by nine, Molly'd eat his sofa. That didn't leave long for small talk.

"Terr, thinking ain't never been your strong suit."

He grinned as Darrell lit up, took a long slow drag, and blew the smoke from that big-assed gee-my-granddaddy-was-an-Indian nose. Fuck, he was still sexy as all get-out.

"Kiss my ass, man," Terrell said. "Last time I checked, you weren't in the running for the Nobel Prize." He damn near choked on his Joe when one pointed boot toe slid up his leg, nudging. "Careful, now," he warned.

"I ain't got time for careful, Terr. I been thinking on you, on the last time I drove through. Took me right on through 'til Denver, that time."

Oh, hell yes. Those words crashed into Terrell's belly, and if he put his coffee cup down a little too hard, no one was saying. "You said you got a room?"

"I did." A ten-spot landed on the table, and Darrell grabbed his hat. "Come on, then. Time's wastin'."

Terrell stood up, towering over Darrell some, liking how he looked wide and broad as the side of a barn next to that tight little butt. He was thinking Darrell might be liking it too, the way the man's biceps went taut and the *click-clack* of them fancy silver-toed boots sped up toward the stairs.

The room wasn't nothing—never was—but it was clean enough, and the bed was right there, along with a little table for a good hat. That hat went spinning about the second Terrell got the door shut and latched, bumping the little lamp they wouldn't turn on. Darrell's hands landed on Terrell's chest with a thud that rocked him, had him bending down to slam their mouths together with a need that squealed and crashed like two semis tying up on the interstate.

Good thing Terrell knew how they were together, how they went off like Saturday night specials in a goat-roper's pocket. He got his shirt unbuttoned fast enough that Terrell didn't tear it, but it was a close thing, those rope-rough hands tugging like he was new corn on the stalk. He went for that pretty buckle, damn near sliced his finger on the thing.

"Motherfucker." Damn, that stung.

"Less talking, asshole. I *need*." Darrell caught his ankle with a boot heel, gave him a good hard shove that had him toppling onto the bed, right on his ass. That asshole was strong for a little banty-rooster fuck.

He'd have bitched too, if it hadn't felt so good, if Darrell's hand hadn't landed with a dull thud on his Johnson and set to rubbing, working him right through the denim. Given the situation, he just nodded and spread like a practiced whore, hips pushing right up as he pulled those too-pretty-for-a-man lips down again. When they got finished tonight, those lips'd be swollen and raw or he'd eat his hat, yessir.

The man tasted like strawberry jelly and smoke and peppermint, which should've been nasty as hell but wasn't, 'cause it tasted like Darrell, and Terrell had been wanting him some of this for going on two years now. He could've got himself all tied up in thinking about it—about coming and going and leaving and right and wrong and shit—but Darrell growled and grabbed one of his hands, pressing it down on the rough-assed sheets above his head. "Stop it," he said. "You either want it or you don't. No thinking. Give me your other hand."

"Fuck you," snarled Terrell.

"Not tonight. You got it last time. I rode sideways for a week." His wrist was squeezed good and hard, making him ache. "Give me your motherfucking hand, Terr. You need this. Now."

They locked horns, both of them tussling for it, teeth catching where they could. By the time Darrell had him locked up in a hold, they were both hard, sweating, breathing into each other's mouths with a kiss that wouldn't back off or back down. One of them hard hands got his fly open, the jeans like to tear the hair on his thighs plumb off as they got shoved down.

The damned things got caught on the tops of his boots, right about the same spot that Darrell's stopped. He finally wrenched one hand free and got it wrapped good and firm around them both, pumping like he meant it. Those black eyes rolled like a mad bull's, and Darrell growled, damn near biting his lips, bruising him in the kiss. Terrell gave his payback, though, thumb working the man's slit, spreading that bit of slick around and making it burn.

Terrell felt it, curling and settling in his belly, a dull ache that made him twist and push, wanting it away and closer all at once. Those rough fingers started moving, reminding him where every bite was, every fucking bruise. Darrell humped, then fucked Terrell's hand like they were quickstepping, and goddamn but he was right there.

Right fucking there.

His hips snapped, and his teeth clicked right together as Darrell rolled his dice, nuts like stones as he shot. Shit, that was... Yeah.

Damn.

He must've said it out loud because Darrell nodded, hot and damp and heavy on top of him, cock throbbing weakly in his fingers, thighs sliding. "You know it. Shit, my legs are all... Goddamn it."

Watching Darrell cuss and kick at the denim got him tickled, got them both laughing hard. "Shit. That's what I get for acting all macho and shit, Terr. I been practicing tonight for right near three days, and I forgot all about the fucking boots."

That just made it worse, and then they were hooting, Darrell flopping back on the bed, cock slapping that tight-as-a-boar's-backside belly. He half rolled, humming as his prick snugged up against one hip, right as rain.

"You're still a dork, cowboy. Riding ain't fixed that," Terrell said.

"Riding don't fix shit. Riding's just... You know, Terr. You used to know."

Thank God the lights were out. "That was a while ago, man. Before shit happened."

"Yeah. Well. There ain't no accounting for taste, Terr." He could see those eyes, like holes burned into a hide of leather. "You look like a fucking leper."

"Yeah, well, whose fault is that?" Man, the sun was coming up. He had dogs to feed.

"Mine, I reckon." Darrell looked toward the window, turning enough that Terrell could push against the strong back. "I got two hours before I got to go. You sleepy?"

"I can sleep in the grave, cowboy." Terrell leaned forward, lips on the patch of skin right below Darrell's hairline.

"Yeah, that's what I hear. Come on, then. That clock don't wait." Those hips pushed back in a clear offer, and Terrell grinned. That probably depended on what side of the clock you was sitting on, didn't it?

Right now, he'd take it, though, wouldn't he? And he'd blow any eight-second fucking bronc away, least 'til Darrell got to the arena.

"You know it, cowboy. Daylight's burning, and I got shit to do. Let's ride."

That got Darrell to chuckling, the sound ready and rough as a cob, and he let himself start to rocking, let the smooth rub of that tight little ass work its magic against his still-pretty-much-interested cock. His hands did a little exploring, touching belly and cock, pointy hip bones and tight little-bitty nipples. There was a big ol' scar from belly button to bottom rib that caught his index finger's attention, the zigzagging thing traveling right on up. "Bull?"

"Yup," Terrell said. "Went ass over teakettle in Denver." Darrell pushed his hand down to wrap around the long, thin cock waiting on him. Yeah, right. No thinking. "Weren't nothing. Just a spill." Yeah. They all were nothing, 'til they were something. Lord, Darrell was like a little furnace, burning and moving against his hand, that slick wet easing the way some.

His own cock filled up right nice, like it knew that certain stallions only rode through on a blue moon and a prayer and it'd best be ready. "You got stuff?"

"Yeah," Darrell said. "In my wallet. Bought it in Shreveport, in case your number hadn't changed."

"It hasn't." He let Darrell lean away to scrabble for the tossed-off jeans, curling forward to taste the spot right above Darrell's crack. He got a little cry for his troubles, so he got another lick in, let his teeth scrape some like he was trying to scratch an itch. Oh, now. Didn't that just make Darrell buck like somebody'd snuck a burr under the saddle. "Easy now, I ain't ridden hard in a month of Sundays."

Then Terrell licked again, fingers cupping those cheeks,

thumbs sliding to tease Darrell's hole. Just 'cause he hadn't done it in a while didn't mean he'd forgotten how. He kept up, licking and touching and feeling, damn near drowning in it, happy as a dog in water. Every little moan, little strangled cry made it closer to right, made him feel ten feet tall. Darrell rolled a little for him, banty-rooster legs curling up and under so he had a better angle, a better view of what he needed. "Lord, cowboy," Terrell told him. "You're fine as frog hair, I swear it."

Darrell moaned and heated under his hands, the smell of the man enough to make his mouth water. "Don't wanna wait on it no more, Terr. Gimme."

"No more waiting." Terrell took the rubber and slid it on, spitting in his hand and slicking himself right on up. Terrell took a bit of a breath as he lined up, looking at the sight of that line of back, tense and waiting on him, the sunlight just starting to paint that skin with Easter-egg colors. Then Darrell grunted and pushed back, his hole pulling Terrell's prick right in. His head slammed back, eyes rolling, and suddenly Terrell didn't give a good goddamn about the light or the dawn or anything but the way they felt, slamming together like barn doors in a tornado.

Darrell crawled right up the wall, hands splayed as they bounced, the cheap old bed singing their praises as they went at it. Terrell got his hands wrapped around Darrell's waist, tugged good and hard until he couldn't tell where his hips stopped and the other man's ass started.

"My cock. Fuck, Terr. I need. Fucking touch me."

He hooted, managing to get his hand down to pull good and hard. "Greedy bastard."

"So you say. More."

Terrell's teeth found heaven in the curve of Darrell's shoulder, biting deep, leaving a mark where no one would see it. No one but Darrell and him would know it was burning there under the vest and shirt.

Darrell went wild as wet heat sprayed over Terrell's fingers. He bucked hard and squeezed Terrell tight enough that the top of his head near popped off, his cock throbbing and swelling as he lost it.

They sat there for a long minute, Darrell on his lap, his head on Darrell's shoulder, both of them panting like dogs. He felt his heart pound against his ribs, fighting to make more room in there.

Darrell shifted, before his naked back got cold, but not before his thighs started complaining about their position. Terrell handed him a couple of tissues to help with the cleanup work, and he wrapped the condom up real good in them before trashing it. Mary Lou Hinson cleaned these rooms, and it wouldn't do to...

They might have napped a little, or they might have just sat there and breathed. Didn't matter. They got dressed without saying much of nothing, Darrell tossing on jeans and undershirt, fastening up that new buckle. Terrell ghosted his fingers over the bite mark on Darrell's shoulders before the button-up went on top of it.

"You see my new truck, Terr? She's a beaut."

Terrell pulled on his boots, nodded. "I did. You still got that piece-of-shit trailer, though. Some things don't change."

"You know it," Darrell said, and gave him a look, long and steady. "Shift's changed in the restaurant. You want one more cup of coffee 'fore I go?"

He checked his watch, nodded. "Sure, son. I got time for a cup before I get to work. Maybe even a sausage biscuit."

"Well, hell. Lookit you, taking chances. Next thing I know you'll be ordering eggs in the morning."

"You never know, asshole. You just never know."

They filed out, letting the door lock behind them as they headed downstairs toward the smell of coffee and the sunshine pouring in.

GOLD RUSH

Hank Edwards

P aul Rondo looked up from the frame he had been using to sift through the fine silt of the streambed, and eyed the large bear of a man kneeling across the water. He had met Carl Phillips three days before when a tired old man and his two tired old mules had led him to this campsite. During the past few years, Paul had acquired a tall pile of debts, a very tall pile. To pay it off—and flee the creditors who were pursuing him—he had sold himself as an indentured servant to a man who was prospecting a parcel of territory for gold. The rush had hit and thousands were flocking west to strike it rich, or, like Paul himself, to escape their lives in the east.

Carl Phillips bore no resemblance to what Paul had pictured during his weeks' long journey across the barren landscape. He had envisioned an overweight, toothless slob, someone he would dislike on sight and come to hate over the next three years. With this image in mind, Paul had been happily stunned to find that Carl was around six four and big shouldered. He weighed at least 220 pounds, most of that muscle. His cotton trousers rode his lower body like an affectionate whore eager for her pay. Every time he moved along the opposing bank from Paul, the man's pants highlighted every curve and bulge of his bulky frame. He wore his flannel shirt unbuttoned to the waist, exposing a broad chest browned from days in the sun. A thick mat of dark red hair, damp with sweat, was visible in the open V of his shirt. His brilliant blue eyes shone from his face, in great contrast to his full, reddish gold beard, and the dark red hair that fell around his shoulders. His large hair-flecked hands moved skillfully along the stream, scooping dirt and silt and shifting it through the boxed screen in his search for riches.

Paul fought back his sudden, painful erection and went back to work. In the last three days, both Carl and Paul had found two gold nuggets apiece, the same number Carl had found in the six months he had worked his forty acres alone.

"Find anything today?" Carl's deep voice floated smoothly over the stream.

"Nope," Paul replied, glancing up and struggling not to stare. "Nothing yet. But I've got a good feeling."

"Yeah?" Carl squinted over the water at him. "Why's that?"

Paul shrugged. "Just do. Don't you get those feelings? Like something's going to happen?"

Carl nodded and eyed him thoughtfully. "Yep, guess I do."

Paul looked down and fought the urge to lift his head and stare at his "partner" (the word they had agreed upon for their arrangement). Losing his inner battle, he raised his brown eyes, looking carefully through the dark hair that had tumbled into his face, and caught Carl staring at him. Paul thought Carl might have trimmed his beard and mustache the night after he had arrived at the camp. And it seemed the man had made a point of rinsing his mouth and cleaning his teeth after breakfast, too. Was Carl trying to impress him, or was Paul imagining things?

He quickly looked back at his work, thinking of the last two nights and how much of a struggle it had been to sleep beside Carl in the same small tent, the man's sweaty, masculine scent riding Paul's craving like a wild mustang. He had sported a constant raging hard-on both nights and hadn't had a chance yet to steal off by himself and ease his tension.

Carl looked away when Paul raised his eyes and caught him staring. Wouldn't do to have Paul know what kind of thoughts he had been having ever since the younger man had ridden up behind that fool Chester three days ago. Before Paul had arrived Carl hadn't bothered much with his hygiene. But now that he had gotten a look at the man who would be his "partner" for the next three years, he thought he might start to work at his appearance a little more. He knew he was still a good-looking man. The women always flocked around him when he went into town, and he kept himself clean as possible considering his living conditions. But now that Paul had shown up and proved to be five years younger than Carl and just about the best-looking man he had seen for a good many years, he was back to working at his looks.

He had found there weren't many men who were interested in having sex with him, but along his journeys he had come across a few, and they had been good times. But none of those men held a candle to Paul. And here he had just come riding over the hill like some kind of gift, his long brown hair bouncing across his shoulders as he rode up on his golden palomino. With the keen eye of a predator, Carl had watched the younger man dismount: his strong, wiry legs as he swung out of the saddle; the long, thin fingers and sturdy grip as he shook Carl's hand;

the deep, sensual brown eyes shaded by long, dark lashes. Not to mention the bulge of Paul's crotch and the way his pants hugged his high, round butt. It pushed Carl almost over the edge with desire. Yep, Carl thought as he stood up and wiped his hands on his pants, the money he had paid for Paul Rondo had been well spent.

"I'm feelin' a might ripe over here," Carl said casually, turning his back to Paul as he shaded his eyes and looked down along the stream to where it fell a short distance away into a clear, cold pool. "I think I might go have myself a bath." He turned his head and looked over his shoulder, cocking a sun-bleached eyebrow. "You interested?"

Paul nearly choked, but he stood up and, not trusting his voice, nodded.

"All right then," Carl said with a grin. "Let's go. I'll get the towels and soap." He walked back to their tent, feeling Paul's eyes on his ass as he moved. He had worn his tightest pants to show off his physique and to entice Paul into expressing an attraction. But Paul had control; he had to give him that much.

Side by side they walked down to the pool, and Carl dropped the soap and towels on a flat dry rock. Turning to face Paul, he smiled then bent down and unlaced his boots. Paul followed suit, and soon they were standing nude before each other. The blood-gorged members that jutted from their groins more than revealed their mutual attraction.

Paul let his eyes travel over Carl's body, taking in the sight of his muscular hairy chest and the thick, uncut cock that was still filling with blood. The man's dick was massive, thicker around than Paul's grip, and longer than a railroad spike. Paul's mouth watered as he watched it grow longer and harder before his eyes, rising from the patch of dark red hair that surrounded Carl's groin.

"Like what you see?" Carl asked in a low voice.

"Yeah, I do." Paul peered into Carl's eyes and saw the promise of hot, raw sex in them.

"I like what I see, too." Carl's eyes traveled down Paul's body, drinking in every detail. A fine layer of dark hair covered his chest and swirled around his quarter-sized dark-brown nipples. His flat stomach curved down to a patch of brown hair from which his cock had sprung like a jack-in-the-box. Paul's dick was thinner, about three inches in diameter—but long, surely nine inches in length. He was uncut as well, the pink head peeking out from its hood. Paul's massive balls hung low between his thighs. More than anything, Carl wanted to take each succulent nut into his mouth and suck on it while Paul squirmed and groaned above him.

"What do you say?" Carl asked. "Shall we get in?"

"Okay." Paul tore his gaze from Carl's body and with a deep breath jumped into the pool. The cold hit him like a locomotive, pulling the wind from his lungs and immediately deflating his throbbing hard-on. He surfaced and gasped for air, teeth chattering.

Carl laughed as he crouched on the rocks, arms folded over his knees. His cock jutted from his thighs, almost skimming the surface of the water. "Warm enough for you?"

Paul smirked as he wrapped his arms around his shoulders. "I forgot how cold it was. I was a little distracted."

"I bet." Carl slid carefully into the water, gasping a little at the temperature. He glided over to Paul then leaned down and kissed him on the mouth.

Paul smiled up at the man towering before him then reached up and pulled Carl's head down to kiss him again. Carl's beard and mustache prickled along Paul's smooth-shaven face, and his cock hardened again despite the cold water. Their tongues collided and wrestled in each other's mouths, grazing their teeth and eliciting groans from both of them.

Breaking the embrace, Carl looked into Paul's eyes. "Let's clean up then get down to business," he told him. He grabbed the soap and boosted Paul onto the rocks surrounding the pool, then lathered him up, his hands caressing each limb and contour, massaging and squeezing. Paul crouched with his back to Carl and allowed the man to wash his ass, groaning as Carl slipped a thick, blunt finger in and out of his pink, puckered hole. After sliding into the water to rinse off, he washed Carl's body, his slender fingers finding their way inside Carl's ass as well.

When they had finished bathing, they sat on the rocks and kissed for a long time, their tongues rubbing themselves raw with lust. Their hands squeezed and pinched and grappled each other's bodies until Carl finally leaned down and gulped Paul's hard, throbbing cock deep into his throat. Paul gasped and lay on the rocks, closing his eyes as Carl's mouth pistoned up and down his shaft.

Raising his heavy, hairy body, Carl moved his hips up and over Paul's head, slapping his thick cock onto Paul's face. Paul immediately opened his mouth wide and took Carl's dick down his throat. He sucked hungrily on the man's prick, earning a deep, satisfied grunt from Carl.

Paul pulled back the foreskin from the tip of Carl's pole and sucked greedily on the soft, pink, bulbous head. He tasted Carl's precum and drank it down eagerly. Letting the foreskin slip back over the tip, he worked his tongue beneath the sheath of skin and ran it around the head.

Carl skinned the hood back from Paul's cock as well, then touched just the tip of his tongue to the sensitive head and waggled it over the piss-slit, sampling the precum that continued to bubble from Paul's rod like a natural spring. He clamped his lips over the head and sucked fiercely on the tip, leaving it bright red.

"Oh, God!" Paul exclaimed. "That feels so damn good! Oh, yeah, suck it."

Carl eased Paul's legs up and moved his attention to the tight anus he had fingered earlier. He lapped at Paul's twitching hole, earning a few gasps and even more groans. Carl shifted the position of his hips, moving over Paul's chest so that his ass sat right on the younger man's face.

Paul locked his sinewy legs around Carl's shoulders as the man suckled and tongued his asshole, groaning at each prod of Carl's tongue. Pulling his arms up to spread the firm globes of Carl's cheeks wide, Paul exposed the tender hole. He licked and sucked for all he was worth, his saliva matting down the red hair that surrounded the tight, pink entrance to paradise.

In one fluid movement, Carl slipped back to his original position, raised his hips, then slammed his cock deep into Paul's throat, feeling the man choke around the girth of him. He pumped slowly into Paul's mouth, increasing his speed until he steadily humped his face. Feeling the cum build up in his balls, he bucked faster. As he fucked Paul's mouth, he wrapped his fist around the base of Paul's cock and bounced his mouth up and down along his shaft at the same rate. Paul pumped his own hips up off the rock to meet Carl's mouth, and soon they were jacking into each other's mouths in rhythm.

"I'm coming," Paul gurgled around Carl's cock, his hands tangling themselves in Carl's long, red hair. His cock erupted in Carl's throat, spewing load after load of hot, thick cum onto Carl's gut and over his beard and mustache.

Carl grunted deeply and, his lips still locked around Paul's spent cock, shot his own hot wad into Paul's mouth. Paul sucked down as much of the spunk as he could, but there was so much it spilled out over his chin and down his cheeks. He suckled greedily on Carl's slowly softening cock, coaxing the last precious drops of cum from the soft, red tip.

Carl rolled off Paul, and they lay breathless for a few minutes, their bodies warming in the sun.

"You're amazing," Paul finally said.

Carl laughed. "You haven't seen anything yet." He stood up, extending his hand and pulling Paul to his feet. They kissed for a few minutes, each tasting his own cum on the other's tongue, then Carl led Paul to the campsite and spread out some blankets on the grass under a small tree. They lay side by side and explored each other's bodies as they kissed a while longer. Sliding down, Carl lifted Paul's legs and ran his tongue along the man's ass crack.

"Oh, damn," Paul groaned, his hands spreading his cheeks wide to allow Carl better access to his sensitive hole. He had only allowed one other man to have him this way, and he was more than ready to let Carl be the second.

"Goddamn," Carl said as his tongue slithered in and out of Paul's tight asshole. "You have got the tightest hole I've ever come across. You ever taken it up there?"

"Once."

"Okay then, I'll go slow." Carl spat into Paul's hole then leaned over and scooped up a glob of lard Chester had brought with the load of supplies. After greasing up Paul's hole, slipping first two then three fingers deep inside the man, he slicked up his long, thick tool.

Carl sat up and positioned himself at the threshold of Paul's ass then looked up at him. "You ready for it?"

"Yeah, do it," Paul said and took in a quick breath as Carl eased himself slowly, carefully inside.

"Everything okay?" Carl asked gently, his cock halfway inside Paul.

"Oh, God," Paul groaned. "It's great." He reached up and pulled Carl down to kiss him hard and deep as Carl slipped in and out of the young man's firm ass, going deeper with each stroke. After several thrusts, Carl plunged completely into him then pulled nearly all the way out before diving right back in.

Paul threw his head back and closed his eyes, his mouth gaping wide open with each thrust of Carl's mammoth cock. He reached down and pulled on his own hard prick, working up another giant load.

Carl looked down and watched Paul's slender fingers work his cock in rhythm with Carl's thrusting. Close to the point of no return, Carl drove deeper into Paul, the wiry hair surrounding his cock brushing Paul's big soft balls as they bounced in time to his thrusts.

With a guttural growl, Carl felt his control skitter away and closed his eyes as his body took over and emptied his load deep inside Paul's tight pink hole. He breathed deeply and leaned back, his cock still buried inside Paul, his hips slowly moving in an unconscious rhythm.

Paul suddenly gasped, and Carl saw his balls pull up close to his body. Leaning forward, still buried inside Paul, Carl caught the first shot of Paul's load in his mouth. The second landed on his cheek and nose, and the rest flew down his throat as he finally got his lips around the cockhead and sucked Paul the rest of the way off.

Carl's cock slipped free of Paul's ass. He slurped up the last of Paul's spunk then reached down to squeeze the last of his own from his softening prick.

After a time, they headed back to the pool and washed up again. Exhausted, they crawled into the small tent they shared and fell asleep in the shade of a tree as the stream babbled past, whispering of hidden treasures yet to be discovered.

DRIFT-FENCE DESPERADO

Julia Talbot

Winter could be cruel in the Texas panhandle. Danny Elam knew that for sure. They'd had a winter just a few years ago, back in 1884, when about three hundred head of the boss's cattle keeled over and died because they got logjammed up on the high end of the drift fence and couldn't figure out how to move on.

Them bovines were right dumb. Almost as stupid as a man who volunteered for winter camp duty, riding up and down that fence all day long. Rain and ice alternated with weirdly warm days where the sun made a man sleepy. The off and on of it was enough to give a man chilblains on some days and fevers on another.

The fence stretched on for miles and miles, an endless march of cedar posts and barbed wire, all set two long paces apart and strung with three strands. The piece Danny patrolled was nigh on fourteen miles long, and that seemed long enough in the middle of a storm, for sure.

He'd been riding two days and was on his way back to his line shack when he spotted the break in the fence. Goddamn sumbitch. Stiff as an old rope, Danny climbed off his gelding and slogged over to look. Cut, clean as a whistle. Didn't look like they'd lost any cattle, but there was a set of horse tracks, shod, plain as day. They headed in, not out. Whatever snake had cut the fence was looking to round up mavericks, no doubt.

Damn it. He was out of supplies and cold to the bone. He marked the location with a big old strip of red flannel, just in case they got snow on top of ice, and headed back home, figuring on coming out in the morning and patching the fence.

Smoke curled out of his stovepipe, and Danny cursed again at the sight. He'd put out that fire when he left two days back, so someone had started it up again. Someone not him, damn it.

He tended his horse first. There was a rawboned gray in his little lean-to, a mare, and it didn't have no brand on it. Old man Flint branded all of his mounts. Danny drew his rifle out, leaving the horses cozying up and his saddle on a post, making for the shack and whoever it was squatting there.

The butt of his rifle hit the planks of the front door hard, making a harsh, ringing sound.

"All right, whoever's in there, come on out. This is my place, and if you so much as twitch about it, I'll blow you to kingdom come."

The door swung open, the stinging wind helping it enough that it banged against the inside wall. Danny's mouth fell open when he saw who stood there. It was like seeing a man come back from the dead.

His old friend Malachi James lifted both hands in the air, giving him a tiny little smile, a curl of the lips so familiar it was like a kick in the gut. "Well, hey there, Danny. How's it hanging?"

Hands lax on his rifle, Danny stood and stared until Malachi stepped back and motioned him in like he was a guest. Then he snapped out of it, stepping inside and carefully setting the long gun in its rack by the door. He took off his hat and hung it up, removed his slicker to shake out.

Then he turned and took one quick step forward so he could jab Malachi right on his square jaw. Pow.

Malachi staggered back, hand coming up to feel where Danny'd hit him, but he didn't fight back, just looked at Danny with them sad, dark eyes, floppy brown hair falling in his face.

"I suppose I deserved that," Malachi said. "I surely do."

"That and more, but I ain't got the energy," Danny returned. "Don't reckon you made coffee?"

"I did." Malachi grabbed his tin cup and poured a measure of hot coffee into it, handing it over. "Got in last night. I fixed the latch when I was warm, so you don't need to worry about the door shutting."

"Well, I'd say thank you if you weren't a low-down thief."

He couldn't believe it. Malachi. Here. In his line shack, looking tired and ragged, but safe and solid and real.

"Now, Danny. You know I didn't steal them horses," Malachi said, watching him close as he sipped his coffee.

"No, but you cut a hole in the fence. What's that for if not for rustlin'? And besides, you ran."

Malachi's face darkened. "I ran because if I'd told them where I was that night they would've strung us both up. Old man Flint wouldn't hold with what we were up to. I'll help you fix the fence tomorrow."

Tomorrow. Jesus. Suddenly too worn down to care, Danny shrugged, setting his coffee aside and stripping down to his union suit. "You can stay the night, at least. We'll go from there. I'm too tired to jaw. Night, then."

Keenly aware of Mal's eyes on him, Danny threw on his slicker and boots and went to the necessary before coming back and curling up on his pallet, right near the fire. He wasn't gonna talk on it no more.

Maybe if he closed his eyes and slept he'd wake up and find it was just a dream.

He dreamed about hangings. Malachi's, in fact, his old friend kicking in the wind, an accusing glare leveled on Danny the whole time.

When he started awake the fire cast only the most sullen glow, the dark right before dawn on them. Someone snuggled right up to his back, warm and long and lean, feeling as good as anything had—except for the hand on his cock, rubbing him through the worn, soft wool of his long johns.

"Mmm," he murmured. "Mal."

"Uh-huh. Missed you, Danny."

His eyes popped open wide, and Danny struggled out of Malachi's embrace, going up on his knees to look down. "What in God's name are you doin', Malachi? Ain't we had enough trouble?"

"No. I think we can borrow a bit more." A lunge brought Malachi right to him, eyes insanely dark this close, lips hard as they took his own.

The fight went right out of him, and Danny kissed Mal right back, hands sliding up to cup the back of Mal's neck, holding him close. So long. It had been so damned long. The kiss went like a battle, his tongue pushing into Mal's mouth to taste, Mal chasing it back into his own mouth. Danny felt his lips bruise and swell, felt the bottom one split under the pressure.

Fingers sliding over the bruise on Malachi's jaw, Danny kissed Mal's cheeks, then down his throat, a frustrated growl leaving him as he encountered cloth. They needed more of the naked, he figured, and he put his thoughts into action, tugging at flannel and wool, the scent of aroused male surrounding them as the clothes fell away.

Malachi felt leaner, Danny thought; his ribs were sticking out a little, but hard muscle still roped his arms and chest, still flexed under the skin of his hips and thighs. Danny explored it all. He'd figured he'd never have this again, not ever. Not with Malachi or anyone else. It was like a gift he couldn't turn down.

His mouth followed his hands, sliding down Malachi's chest, over the dark, flat nipples, right down the hard breastbone, all the way down the now concave belly where a trail of black hair pointed the way. Finally he just gave in and took what he wanted, putting his mouth on Malachi's cock, tongue stroking over the loose skin at the head, lips closing around it and sliding down.

A deep groan was his reward, Malachi bucking under his mouth, and Danny almost smiled. He remembered the first time Mal had ever done that to him. He'd never thought of a mouth on that part of him, hadn't even been able to imagine the pleasure it would bring.

Now he knew. Sinking deeper on Mal's cock, Danny sucked, putting a year of lonely nights into it, his hand coming up to cup Mal's heavy balls, pushing against them slightly.

Malachi cursed, the sound sharp and rough, before reaching down to grab Danny, turning him so his hips were level with Mal's mouth. Now they both felt it, they both had the heat and wet of it as Malachi's tongue slid along the underside of Danny's cock, playing it expertly. His belly went hard as a board, his ass clenching, and Danny moaned, riding it for all he was worth.

When one calloused finger pushed along his crease and poked at his hole, Danny did his best to relax, letting it in. He

222

COWBOYS

opened up, rode back on it, and next thing he knew Malachi's finger was curling in him, finding a sweet, sweet spot inside him and pressing it. Everything in him zinged, making him buck into Malachi's mouth, making him cry out around the flesh in his mouth. When he shot his load it really was like a little death, draining him, leaving him spent and panting.

Danny made no resistance when Malachi turned him over, pulling him up on his knees, that wet, hot tongue pushing at his hole, opening him even more, getting him slick. And when Malachi slid inside him, thick and hard and hot as a poker from the fire, all he could do was moan and take it, his body trying to wake up again, his cock twitching madly.

Malachi rode him like a bank robber's horse, until they were both nearly lathered, the little cabin heating up until Danny was sure it was gonna start melting the ice outside. In and out, that heavy cock thrust and prodded until he was braced on his elbows, pushing back for all he was worth, Malachi's hand on his reawakened prick, pulling in time. When they came, they came together. Malachi filled him with hot seed, his own cock jerking almost dry after the first load he'd shot, the pleasure as big as the Texas sky.

They lay together a long time, until light started creeping in around the door, and Danny stirred. Malachi put a hand on his hip to hold him.

"Come with me, Danny. I came back for you. Riding the trail wasn't the same without you."

A quick roll had him facing Malachi, staring straight into those sloe eyes. "It'll make me an outlaw too, Mal. And I ain't done nothin' wrong." He hated to be the one to put the sad back on that face, the lines around Mal's eyes and nose deepening.

"I haven't either. You know that."

"I know."

They looked at each other, neither of them willing to beg. Oh, they'd had them a time when they rode together, loving every night, laughing during the day. He had him a good job now with Mr. Flint and the Bar D, had a good life. What kind of life would he have on the run?

"Well, even if you ain't coming, I got to get going. Want me to help you with that fence?" Malachi asked.

"You damn betcha."

They didn't say much after that, just got up and took turns going out, then ate some hardtack and jerky. Danny thought on it, though, thought hard and long, and while Malachi was out saddling the horses, he packed up his few belongings and his little stash of greenbacks, stuffing it all in his saddlebags and tying up a bedroll. The fire just took a load of icy slush to put it all the way out, and the little shack was clean as a whistle.

If Malachi noticed the extra Danny carried along with his rifle and his slicker, he didn't say so, but when Danny rode with him right through the hole in the fence, Malachi finally broke the silence.

"Thought you'd stay on that side," Mal said, looking him right in the eye.

Danny grabbed his tools and headed for the break, shaking his head. "Can't do that if I'm gonna become an outlaw and ride with you, now can I? Come on and help me."

There was a long silence before he heard Malachi's boots hit the ground, the jingle of spurs moving close as Malachi reached for the wire. "An outlaw wouldn't fix a drift fence."

"No, sir." Danny grinned over, figuring he was Mr. Flint's cowboy until the job was done. Once that break was mended, though, he was Malachi's drift-fence desperado for good.

ABOUT THE AUTHORS

SHANE ALLISON is the author of four chapbooks of poetry. His fifth book, *I Want to Fuck a Redneck*, is due out any day now from Scintillating Publications. His poems and stories have appeared in *Savage Lust, Velvet Mafia, Suspect Thoughts, Mind Caviar, Blue Food, Outsider Ink, zafusy, Shampoo, New Delta Review, Mississippi Review, Best Black Gay Erotica*, and *Ultimate Gay Erotica*. He has work forthcoming in *Hustlers: Erotic Stories of Sex for Hire*. He loves nothing more than receiving dirty little notes at starsissy42@hotmail.com.

VICTOR J. BANIS has written professionally since 1963 and has authored more than 140 books. He lives in the Blue Ridge of West Virginia.

A native Californian, **BEARMUFFIN** lives in San Diego with two leather bears in a stimulating ménage à trois. He writes erotica for *Honcho* and *Torso*. His work has also appeared in *Manscape*, *In Touch*, *Hot Shots*, *Friction*, and *Ultimate Gay Erotica*.

STEVE BERMAN has published more than sixty stories and articles. His work appears in anthologies such as *Best Erotic Ghost Stories*, *Best Gay Erotica 2005*, *The Faery Reel*, and *Skin & Ink*. Haworth Press will publish his novel in 2007.

DALE CHASE has been writing gay erotica for eight years and has had more than one hundred stories published in various magazines and anthologies, including translation into German. *Harrington Gay Men's Fiction Quarterly* recently published his first literary story, and his collection of Victorian gentlemen's erotica, *The Company He Keeps*, is due from Haworth Press in 2007. A native Californian, Dale lives near San Francisco and is working on a novel.

DALLAS COLEMAN grew up in deep east Texas surrounded by beef masters, quarter horses, and a helluva lot of goats. He survived. He escaped. He has, thus far, resisted his daddy's attempts to reclaim him. Dallas writes because it's cheaper than therapy.

HANK EDWARDS is the author of the humorous erotic novel *Fluffers, Inc.* More than two dozen of his stories have appeared in various erotica magazines, including *Honcho*, *American Bear*, and *100% Beef* as well as a number of anthologies. Hank lives in a Detroit suburb with his very patient partner of many years and their orange tabby who believes he's a dog. To feed and clothe himself, he organizes software testing for an impersonal multinational corporation. Visit his website at www.hankedwardsbooks.com.

JUDE GRAY is a good ol' boy from a tiny town in Texas. He lives on a small piece of land with his longtime partner and their three dogs. Jude works at a local hardware store where he enjoys stocking tools and taking smoke breaks.

GUY HARRIS grew up in California, where he first learned to ride. He currently lives outside San Francisco, a short drive from the coastal ranches and acres of riding trails along Highway 1. "Pole Inn" is his first published story.

NEIL PLAKCY is the author of *Mahu*, a mystery novel featuring Honolulu police detective Kimo Kanapa'aka. A contributor to *Men Seeking Men, My First Time 2*, and *Dorm Porn*, he's also the editor of a forthcoming anthology from Alyson Books that focuses on gay men and their dogs. Neil received his MFA in creative writing from Florida International University and is a professor of English at Broward Community College.

CB POTTS is a full-time freelance writer from upstate New York. There's a special spot in CB's heart for all things rodeo. Send an email to ctpotts@juno.com or read more of CB's work in *Hot Gay Erotica*, also available from Cleis Press.

DOMINIC SANTI is a former technical editor turned rogue whose latest erotic work is the German language collection *Kerle Im Lustrausch*. His fiction is available in English in *Best Gay Erotica 2000* and *2004, Best of Best Gay Erotica 2, Best American Erotica 2004, Best Bisexual Erotica 1* and *2, Tough Guys, His Underwear*, various volumes in the *Friction* series as well as dozens of other smutty anthologies and magazines, and on the Internet. Visit www.nicksantistories.com.

SIMON SHEPPARD is the author of *In Deep: Erotic Stories, Sex Parties 101, Kinkorama,* and the award-winning *Hotter Than Hell and Other Stories.* He also writes the columns "Sex Talk" and "Perv," and is currently working on a historical survey of gay porn. His work also appears in more than 125 anthologies, including many editions of *Best American Erotica* and *Best Gay Erotica. San Francisco* magazine has called him "our erotica king," but he hasn't let it go to his head. Say hi at www.simonsheppard.com.

JULIA TALBOT has published gay erotica with Torquere Press and Fishnetmag.com, lesbian erotica with Suspect Thoughts Press and Pretty Things Press, and other stories with Changeling Press and in Justus Roux's *Erotica Tales.*

Born in Halifax, raised in Montreal, and currently living in Ottawa, **VIC WINTER** loves winter best of all the seasons and stays warm on cold nights by writing gay erotica. Words and snow, silence and long nights, the fall of rain and of silk, and men in love are some of Vic's other favorite things. To learn more, visit www.stemsandfeathers.org/vwinter.

ABOUT THE EDITOR

TOM GRAHAM lives in Wyoming, with his partner of many years. When he's not writing or editing gay erotica, he spends his time taking care of his ranch and two young sons, David and Chance.